ZANE'S TRACE

Zane
belongs
Zanesville.

her

the

Love
is
the

Zanesv

for

answer.

ZANE'S TRACE

ALLAN WOLF

CANDLEWICK PRESS

Copyright © 2007 by Allan Wolf

First paperback edition 2010

The Library of Congress has cataloged the hardcover edition as follows:

Wolf, Allan.
Zane's trace / by Allan Wolf. —1st ed.
p.   cm.
Summary: Believing he has killed his grandfather, Zane Guesswind heads for his mother's Zanesville, Ohio, grave to kill himself, driving the 1969 Plymouth Barracuda his long-gone father left behind, and meeting along the way assorted characters who helps him discover who he really is.
ISBN 978-0-7636-2858-1 (hardcover)
[1. Death—Fiction. 2. Automobile travel—Fiction. 3. Coming of age—Fiction.
4. Family—Fiction. 5. Epilepsy—Fiction. 6. People of mixed race—Fiction.
7. Orphans—Fiction.]   I. Title.
PZ7.W8185513Zan 2007
[Fic}—dc22   2007024187

ISBN 978-0-7636-4378-2 (paperback)

10   12   14   13   11   09
RRC
2   4   6   8   10   9   7   5   3   1

Printed in Crawfordsville, IN, U.S.A.

This book was typeset in PMN Caecilia.

Candlewick Press
99 Dover Street
Somerville, Massachusetts 02144

visit us as www.candlewick.com

For Daisy

Suddenly the fingers of a human hand appeared

and wrote on the plaster of the wall, near the

lampstand in the royal palace. The king watched

the hand as it wrote. His face turned pale and he

was so frightened that his knees knocked together

and his legs gave way.

Daniel 5:5–6

DRAMATIS PERSONAE

ZANE HAROLD GUESSWIND
A seventeen-year-old boy driving a stolen 1969 Plymouth Barracuda

LIBBA
Zane's passenger, a mysterious teenage girl

ELIZABETH BELL GUESSWIND
Zane's schizophrenic mother

STANLEY GUESSWIND
Zane's absent father

EARL BELL
Zane's bitter grandfather, who suffers a stroke

BETTY ZANE
A frontier heroine during the Revolutionary War

BEAR BREAKS THE BRANCH
Zane's vengeful Indian ancestor

RICHARD SHADBURN
A stagecoach driver and escaped slave

ZACHARY GUESSWIND
Zane's responsible older brother, a deputy sheriff

KITTY AND CALLIOPE
Zane's friends; a rebellious, reckless boy and an intelligent, cautious girl

WES COULTTER
A dim-witted bully

EXTRAS
A diner cashier, a McDonald's drive-through attendant,
a motel desk clerk, a psychiatrist, and a state trooper

SETTING

A tangle of highways and back roads from Baltimore, Maryland,
to Zanesville, Ohio. A diner. Two McDonald's drive-through windows.
Two graveyards. A motel. And a funeral home.

I-70 West: Mile Marker 82
* 334 Miles to Zanesville

When I die
I want to come back
as a 1969 Plymouth Barracuda
midnight blue with black-tape accents,
twin dummy hood scoops,
and a 440 big-block engine
stuffed between the fenders.
An engine so big they had to install it
with a shoehorn and a hammer.

I've got a six-pack of Mountain Dew,
a book bag filled with Pop-Tarts, a jumbo pack
of Sharpies, a change of socks,
fifty dollars cash, a credit card in my wallet,
and a loaded gun in the trunk.
No rearview mirror. And no more worries.
It's just over three hundred miles to Zanesville, Ohio.

A straight shot.

Gotta make good time.
The sun's already up.
By now they've probably
found the old man's body.

I-70 West: Mile Marker 80

My mother used to read me this book,
Harold and the Purple Crayon.
Harold was a little kid who made
anything happen just by drawing it.
He could draw a horizon, or a window,
or a door, or stairs, or stars, or a boat,
or a spaceship. No trouble existed
that Harold couldn't fix.

                        A few years later
Mom kept getting sicker, so Grandpa moved
in with us for good. That's when I started
writing on my bedroom walls.

Harold had a purple crayon. I've got Sharpies—
medium-tip mostly,
the occasional king size for big ideas.

I figured I could make everything work out
if I just wrote on my walls. If I just wrote
the right phrase the right number of times
or in the right color.

    Give my mother back her mind.
    Calm the demons in her head.

Leave the darkness far behind.
If need be, take me instead.

My Wyandot shaman father was not
around to give me spiritual guidance.
So I created my own heaven, Zane-atopia,
and I drew a picture of it on my ceiling.
    Zane-atopia existed at the top of
    Mount Guesswind, and my life was the climb.
    The earthly world was a dragon's tail
    wrapped around the mountain's base. The bad times
    were dark clouds. The good times a rainbow.
    A bright flash of light shone at the tip-top point
    of the mountain (where good people went
    to live with God) and inside the light was my mom
    and my brother, Zach, and Stanley (he's my dad),
    and even the old man.

All of this I drew on the ceiling
until my arms were like lead pipes
and my neck was a train wreck.

But it felt good in my stomach.
Like Michelangelo must have felt
painting the Sistine Chapel. Like reaching
up to touch God's fingertip.

3

Now my walls are whispering ten miles back.
I'll never draw on them or write on them again.
But I can't help looking at the Barracuda's dash:
an empty space waiting to be filled.
These Sharpies are dependable.
The only thing I can count on.
They'll write on just about anything.

The thought of it
makes my fingertips itch.

I-70 West: Mile Marker 79

I never did belong in Baltimore.
It hit me like the voice of God
a few weeks ago, with summer break
gasping to an end:
>*You don't belong, Zane.*
>*You don't belong.*
I wrote it on my walls all day.
>*Don't belong. Don't belong. Don't belong.*
Till I got fed up and Googled myself.
And there it was, just a couple pages in:
"Zanesville, Ohio—population 25,586.
Home of the world's only Y-Bridge."
A bridge where three roads intersect!

A town named after me
with a bridge that asks, *Why, why, why?*
I drew the bridge. I drew myself in its center.
And I gave it a caption. I inked it into my walls.
>*Zane belongs in Zanesville.*
>*Zanesville is the place for Zane.*
Why had I not thought of it before?
Zanesville is the town where Mom is buried.

I may as well be buried there too.

I-70 West: Mile Marker 77

Give my mother back her mind.
Calm the demons in her head.
Leave the darkness far behind.
If need be, take me instead.

The day I began to write on my walls
I was listening to the old man
hound my mother in his usual way.

Ee-liz-a-beth, this. Ee-liz-a-beth, that.

My grandfather's voice carried down
the air ducts to my basement bedroom,
poisoning the stillness, dimly lit.
The floor was gray cement, the walls light blue,
the ceiling bright white and easy to reach.
I was lying on my bed flipping a penny
and considering my options—
       should I smother the old man with a pillow?
       or plunge a knife into his black heart?
heads, tails, tails, heads, tails, heads—
when the penny took a wild hop,
fell between the bed and the wall,
and lodged in a gap behind the baseboard.

And just like that, it had disappeared.

6

Ee-liz-a-beth, this. Ee-liz-a-beth, that.

That's when I heard the music in my head.
Music like a windup jack-in-the-box ready to pop.
This was the first of the usual signs:

A seizure was on its way.

I-70 West: Mile Marker 75

I knew from experience
I had about five minutes
till the seizure hit.

    Ee-liz-a-beth, this. Ee-liz-a-beth, that.

I broke into a sweat. I felt dizzy.
I began to hear the voices.
My mother. My brother. The old man.
All of them calling to me.
But they weren't there.

The penny is hidden, I thought.
Hidden behind the baseboard.
No one will know. Only me.
My responsibility.

I had to tell.
                  Someone had to know.

Not about the seizure,
not about my mother, but the penny.

So I pulled my bed away from the wall.
And very carefully. Very lightly,

8

in pencil, just above the spot
where the penny had gone, I wrote:

Penny lost here by Zane Harold Guesswind.

Just like that the panic was gone.
It almost felt as if that penny
had been trapped inside of me.
Or maybe I felt I *was* the penny.
Or maybe it's all the same.

Whatever it was, the simple act of writing
on my wall had strengthened me somehow.

I went through my usual routine.
Called up the stairs to Grandpa and Mom.
Removed my shoes. Spit out my gum.
And despite myself, I savored this moment:
the twilight zone between the onset and the blackout.
I climbed into bed as I always did
to wait for the seizure to hit . . .

but the seizure never came.
Just that once, it didn't come.
The voices in my head faded.

The jack-in-the-box music came to an end.
And for an instant my grandfather ceased
his bickering through the ductwork.
Alone in my room. My walls whispered to me.
Hummed to me. Soothed me.
I read what I had written:

    Penny lost . . . Zane Harold Guesswind . . .
       . . . lost here . . . lost . . .

Then I got out of bed,
and I wrote some more. And I wrote
for a couple hours. Pencil at first.
Then crayons. Then watercolor markers.
Then permanent markers.
These last gave the most satisfaction.
The ink so vivid and real.
The ink so here-to-stay real.
So I-will-never-leave-you real.
It seeped in and spread just slightly,
binding itself into the pores
of the whispering wall forever.

I felt how Harold must feel
when he's drowning in the sea
and draws himself a boat.

I-70 West: Mile Marker 72

All through junior high I wrote on my walls.
I drew pictures too, but mostly I wrote—
whatever babble would come out of me.
Some of it made sense:

> *Give my mother back her mind.*

> *I itch because my skin doesn't fit.*

Most of it made no sense:

> *Don't get whole-stung by a half-bee.*

> *The Bongo Boys eat flesh behind the Red Barn!*

I wrote out extensive dialogues
because—hell—life all sounds like a screenplay to me:

Space Alien:	Cheer up, young Earthling, for these are the best years of your life.
Me:	Then why do I feel like a lobster in a holding tank at a seafood restaurant?
Grandpa:	How do you like my new hearing aid?
Me:	Nice, Grandpa. What kind is it?
Grandpa:	It's about nine thirty.
Space Alien:	Waiter? I'll be having that lobster now.

Using a few tubes of Crazy Glue
and a bin of Zachary's and my old toys,
I began to add objects for a 3-D effect:
a tiny plastic stagecoach pulled by plastic horses
running up one wall. Hanging upside down

from the ceiling, Indians attacking
a Lincoln Log fort. Toy armies facing off—
guns, tomahawks, bows and arrows, and scalps.
A red Sharpie made the men bleed.
And I wrote and I wrote and I wrote.
The worse Mom got, the more I wrote.
The more the old man nagged her,
the more I wrote. And the more empty
spaces I filled, the better I felt.

The penny
behind the baseboard
writing its way out.

Besides myself, Kitty and Calliope were
the only other people to write on my walls.
Kitty, despite his name, is a boy.
He is overweight. He dresses in black, always.
He wears black eyeliner; dyes his hair black too.
Calliope is a super-smart, chic-geek, beautiful girl
who could have any guy she wanted
if she didn't refuse to dumb herself down.
Regardless of my seizures and my bizarre family,
Kitty and Calliope have been constant friends.

They were with me the day I drew
the funny picture of Grandpa,
a big cartoon hammer smashing his head.
Next to the picture I had written *BOING!*
We all laughed.
Then a couple days later . . . Grandpa has a stroke
that paralyzes half his body and garbles his speech.

I flipped out, but Kitty and Calliope
called me melodramatic.
They say it was just a coincidence.

I'm not so sure.

I-70 West: Mile Marker 68

*. 320 Miles to Zanesville

In eighth grade, not long after Grandpa's stroke,
I was assigned my own personal, full-time bully,
a badly drawn cartoon of a bully named Wes Coultter:
thick neck, white short-sleeved T-shirt,
sleeves rolled up, baggy blue jeans and a crew cut.

He picked on me relentlessly.
And I would not fight, which made it worse:

> Wes: Yo, in-Zane! How da hell ya doin'?
> Me: Fine, Wes. How the hell are you today?
> Wes: Duh, I feel like poundin' yer face in!
> Me: Now, now, Wes. Use your words.
> Wes: Okay, in-Zane, I'll use my woids. My woids say
>   yer a freak!

Perhaps had I punched him back just once,
we would have become best buddies.
In books and on television, the wimp
eventually stands up to the bully.
Not so in my case. Conflict terrified me.

Kitty and Calliope were no help at all.
And Zach was dating Wes's
older sister, Susan, for Christ's sake!
My strategy was to lay low for a couple years

and wait for Wes to move away.
Finally I tried writing it on my walls:

> Wes Coultter, *you gotta go.*
> Wes Coultter, *you cannot stay.*
> Wes Coultter, *you gotta go.*
> Wes Coultter *must move away.*

Then, the very next week . . . he did.

Grand Mal.

That's the name for the most extreme seizure.
In earthquake terms, it's a 10 on the Richter scale.
Grand Mal means Big Bad (as in Big Bad Wolf).
And Big Bad Wolf is how I picture it:
my eyes roll back into my head;
my bones creak; my muscles stretch;
my jaw juts out; my nose sprouts hair;
claws form on my feet and hands.
I can only imagine it, of course,
because I'm unconscious during that part.
But the evidence is there when I wake up,
on the faces of those in the room forced to watch.
I feel like the werewolf who forgets
he's a mutant and goes for a walk in the moonlight.

Despite taking medication twice a day,
the first week of my freshman year, in the middle
of the lunchroom floor, I went *Grand Mal.*

    Kitty, Calliope, and I were all attending
    high school at Arkham Asylum
    for the Criminally Insane—the same
    place they keep the Joker, the Riddler, and Two-Face.
Wes Coultter had thrown mashed potatoes at me.
"Pop Goes the Weasel" started plinking

in my ears. The lunchroom floor shifted
like a wave. Voices began to bounce
in my brain. I approached the nearest teacher.
And I tried to speak calmly.

> Me: My name is Zane Guesswind. In four or five
> minutes I'm going to have a seizure. I'm going to
> begin to shake violently. I need you to hold me
> down on the floor so I don't hurt myself or
> someone else. And please call my brother to let
> him know. Here's his card.

Then I lay down on the floor
and I went *Grand Mal*.

I-70 West: Mile Marker 64

* 316 Miles to Zanesville

When I regained consciousness, I couldn't
remember who I was or where I was,
or how I came to be on the floor, why
I ached from head to toe, or why a teacher
was looming over me, holding my arms—
his face screwed up in sweaty horror.
Or why a crowd of teenagers surrounded me,
each one wearing the same expression
of curious revulsion, as if they
were gathered around a two-headed calf.

Seizures are bad. Big bad. *Grand Mal.*
But even worse is the fear you live with afterward.
The fear that it will happen again.
And worst of all is other people's fear—
their fear is more unbearable than your own.
And their looks of pity and loathing.

Nearly every member of the freshman class
had been there for the show. I woke up
from a wild demonic trance, clothes torn,
up to my elbows in gore, beside the half-eaten gazelle
robbed from the zoo in the night.

So much for finding a date to the prom.

I-70 West: Mile Marker 62

✳ 314 Miles to Zanesville

Baltimore's half an hour behind.
Frederick's coming up next. After that
come Hagerstown, Cumberland, Washington,
and Wheeling. Then on and on to Zanesville
(that's where a boy named Zane belongs)
and I'm making good time, thanks to Betsy.
Betsy's what I call the Cuda.
Sounds like Mom:

> *Heavens to Betsy!* this.
> *Heavens to Betsy!* that.

The car just sat there after Mom died.
Zachary paid someone to clean the interior.
He tinkered with the engine some
and he kept the tags up-to-date.
But he didn't drive it much himself.
Said it reminded him too much of Mom.
Mom hadn't liked to drive it either.
Said it reminded her too much of Stanley.
The old man drove it some, until the stroke.
Until I drew the hammer going *BOING*.
Now Stanley, Mom, the old man—all of 'em gone.
Zach is flossing his teeth back in Baltimore.
And here I am in the Cuda's front seat.
I planned it all out. Interstate 70
will take me to Zanesville, no turns,

no detours, no possible way of getting lost,
a straight shot.

It was the last thing I wrote
on my walls before I left the house.
The last thing I'll write on my walls. Ever.

One straight shot.

I-70 West: Mile Marker 60

* 312 Miles to Zanesville

The mile markers flash by, a steady,
silent countdown. The Cuda runs smooth.
This car and I have been to Zanesville once before.
When I was six. We went to Zanesville to bury
my grandmother (whom I had never met)
in the family plot. (Don't ask me why a family
from Baltimore, Maryland, has a family
plot in Zanesville, Ohio.)

               Mom dressed
Zach and me in little black suits. She dressed
herself in yellow. So we looked like two
Secret Service agents (one of them a midget)
flanking a big daffodil.
             All the white
mourners hated us. Luckily there were only
two of them. The other two mourners were black:
the Shadburns from Cleveland.

                  And that's how
my brother and I found out Grandma Katie
had been African American.
I hadn't even known her name. Neither
the old man nor Mom had ever brought it up.
Turns out Grandma Katie had run away from Cleveland

during the Depression and passed herself off
as a white woman.

After the funeral

I sat in the backseat of the Cuda
on the long trip home. Zach was in front.
The conversation went like this:

> Zach: You mean to tell me we're part black?
> Mom: Does it matter?
> Zach: Well, hell yes. I'm sixteen, Mom. I need to
> know.

That's how Zach is. He always needs to know.

Turns out the old man did *not* know
that his bride, Grandma Katie, was black—
not until after he'd married her;
and not until long after Mom was born.
When Grandpa finally *did* find out,
Grandma Katie left. Left the old man
and my mother behind—and never came back.

The old man did not come to the funeral.
Mom asked him if he wanted to.

> Grandpa: Better that bitch had never been born.

Years later, on my walls, I would draw
The Zane Family Tree:

Grandparents:	Earl Bell and Katie Shadburn
Parents:	Elizabeth Bell and Stanley Guesswind
Children:	Zachary and Zane

A half-dead stump.
A single branch.
And two lone leaves.

Stanley, my father, was an alcoholic
who walked out on us after one of my mother's
botched suicides. A few months later
Zach got the call telling us Stanley had died
on somebody's couch in New York City.
When I grew up, I recorded it on my wall.

Stanley did an Edgar Allan Poe.

I'm told Mom and Zach both took it bad.

Mom said he was some sort of Wyandot shaman.
Like an Indian priest. She really loved him.
Loved him to the end. I say he was just an asshole.

Stanley left behind three things: A broken-down
lawn mower; the Plymouth Barracuda;
and a real, no-shit, antique flintlock handgun
that still works. If Stanley wasn't lying,
the gun is an old British dueling pistol.
One of Stanley's Wyandot ancestors
(hence one of *my* ancestors) used the gun
to kill white people during the last battle
of the Revolution.

According to Zach
the pistol had a name: the Fool's Fire-Hand.
Before the end of my sophomore year
my mother used it to kill herself.
She's buried in the Zanesville family plot.
I refused to go to the funeral.

With Mom gone and the old man half-paralyzed,
my brother, Zachary, moved back in.
Zachary is a mechanic, just like the old man was.
    Those guys could fix *any* car.
Zach is also a deputy in the local sheriff's office.
Deputy Zach is ten years older than me.
    Very responsible. Flosses his teeth *every* night.
Not nearly as messed up as the rest of us.
He lets me spend my time doing pretty much
whatever I want so long as I don't skip school
and don't break the law. Best of all,
Zach doesn't care if I write on my walls.

Zach wanted to get rid of the pistol
but I wanted to keep it for myself.
My state-appointed shrink (thank you, DSS)
convinced my brother it would be okay.

> Dr. Nutsucker: Since Zane refused to attend his
> mother's funeral, he is doubtless
> suffering from closure issues.
> Perhaps keeping the weapon will
> help him to cope with his loss and
> move him more smoothly through
> the necessary stages of the grieving
> process.

Deputy Zach: You mean you want me to help my
                      kid brother grieve by giving him a
                      gun? Are you nuts?
Dr. Nutsucker: Perhaps, Zach, you are suffering from
                      closure issues of your own, eh? I
                      want you to think about that.

Zach finally agreed and brought home the gun
(the Fool's Fire-Hand, our family heirloom)
but not before he had "fixed it" so it wouldn't shoot.
I fixed it back so it would (thank you, vocational machine
    shop).
Then I added it to the wonder of my walls—
    carved a hole in the gypsum
    to accommodate the gun barrel
    and I shoved it in—
where it sat for months
pistol grip out,

    helping me to grieve.

I-70 West: Mile Marker 55

I don't remember exactly when
I hatched my master plan: to shoot
myself at my mother's grave. It was one
of those crazy ideas that seems like a joke—
at first.

      I am going to Zanesville
to *bring closure to the grieving process:*

BANG!
      Perhaps Mom will be waiting for me
on the other side, with a glass of milk
and a heavenly PBJ on a plate.

I figure it's six or seven hours
from my bedroom to the family plot.
I'll find Elizabeth Guesswind's grave,
and I'll hold the pistol under my chin,
the way she did. Even for me the idea
is way over the top. Kitty and Calliope
would call it melodrama. The scheme
remained just a fantasy of mine

until last night, when I made the old man die.
When I crossed him off the family tree
and smudged him from Zane-atopia's light.

After that the die was cast.

I did not kill him directly, yet I
was certainly the cause.
                              Last night—
the Zane-atopia scene on my ceiling,
the flash of light at the top of Mount Guesswind,
the heaven holding Mom, Stanley, Zach, me,
and Grandpa?
                    I smudged the old man out
with a fat, black marker—king size.
Last night I erased the old man from the light.

I was hating him so much. I wanted him
to disappear. How is it that Grandpa's stroke
had been so easy, but no matter how many
hours I wrote, I could not save my mom,
or bring her back to life?

                        Last night, I'm looking
up to my ceiling, at Zane-atopia—
with its dopey dragon and clouds and rainbows
and mountains and light—with all the same
questions still asking themselves in my head:
Who chooses that the old man stays while my mother
is gone forever? Who chooses that Grandpa
lingers here, smelling like piss and cigarettes,
handing me cash and trying to be my friend?

This man who treated my mother like garbage?
Why is Earl Bell the trunk of our twisted
family tree at all?

    And so I smudged him
from the light, and I smudged him off the tree
trunk too. Under the trunk's black smudge was the lone
name, Katie Shadburn, my closest ancestor,
a total stranger.
          Then I flushed my seizure
pills down the toilet. And I slept. And as I slept,
the old man slipped away.

I-70 West: Mile Marker 48
✳ 300 Miles to Zanesville

So that's how the old man died last night, sitting
in the La-Z-Boy in front of the television.
I found him this morning before sunup,
cigarette with a long gray ash in his hand.
Probably hadn't taken a drag. Oxygen tubes
disappeared up each nostril. His dead eyes open.
A *Wheel of Fortune* rerun on the TV.
A smiling contestant buying a vowel.

It was me—my walls and I—that killed him.

I-70 West: Mile Marker 43
✳ 295 Miles to Zanesville

I had to go. And go quick.

Zanesville, Ohio—population 25,586.

Home of the world's only Y-Bridge.

It was sooner than planned, but then why the hell not?

They will read my walls. They will see it's my fault.

Zanesville is the place for Zane.

How to get there? *Bike downtown. Buy a bus ticket.*

How to buy it? *Credit card.*

Zach is asleep as I go through his wallet.

Credit card. Bingo!

Then on to Grandpa's closet,

where I suspect the old man keeps his cash.

A few times I have seen him

leaning over the big square box,

but I had never opened it myself.

And I had not read—until this moment—

the label on the box's top:

Elizabeth Bell Guesswind: Personal Articles

Mom's stuff from the police investigation.

The things she had with her when she died.

I-70 West: Mile Marker 39

I lift off the lid.
A set of car keys catches my eye.
I recognize them at once—Plymouth Barracuda.

> *Change of plan. I go back for Zach's wallet.*
> Now I'll be needing a driver's license too.

The rest of the box *I'll go through later.*
For now *I'll set it on the passenger seat.*
The flintlock pistol *I'll pull from my wall and pack in the*
   trunk.
I will be needing it—

   One straight shot—

wanting it, once I get to Zanesville.

And I drive
away from my sleeping brother. I drive
away from Arkham Asylum
and my father's broken lawn mower. I drive
away from my mother's sobbing. I drive
away from the whispering walls and medication,
and Zane-atopia and Grandpa smudged from the light.

I drive away from the La-Z-Boy
and the long gray ash, and the oxygen tank,
and the old man's dead eyes watching
to see where the Wheel of Fortune will stop.

The Happy Days Diner
Near Hagerstown, Maryland

This is when I first see the girl.
I stop to gas up and take a leak.
The Happy Days Diner is attached to the truck stop
and made up to look all retro
(poodle skirts, leather jackets, jukebox).
She is sitting in a booth, alone, crying.
But everyone is acting as if she isn't there.

The woman at the register winks at me.
    That be all, honey?
I buy a Mountain Dew, a cup of black coffee,
and another pack of Sharpies on impulse.

    Me: This and the gas.

As the register woman runs Zach's credit card,
I turn to see the girl in the booth.
She is staring at me.
She looks straight into me,
like she knows everything about me,
like Grandpa and my brother look
at cars they have taken apart
and put back together
a hundred times.

She has a cardboard box
and she begins shoving things into it:
a blue folded blanket, spiral notebooks,
pens and pencils, a dog-eared dictionary,
old photographs, a toothbrush, a book on birds.

I sign the credit card slip:
    Zachary Guesswind.
I walk back to the Cuda
and when I open my door,
there she is, standing on the other side of the car.
She has short, chestnut-brown hair.
Older than me, but not by much.
Not my type but good-looking.
But then what do *I* know?

    She: I could use a lift, if you don't mind.

I don't know what to say.
So she keeps talking.

    She: Which way are you headed?
    Me: Zanesville, Ohio.
    She: Well, that will do.

She laughs and slides onto the passenger seat.

    She: I'm on my way to Zanesville too.

The girl's name is Libba.
Libba starts most of our conversations,
and Libba ends most of our conversations.
She is a have-the-last-word girl.

> She: Who wrote on the dashboard?
>
> Me: What? Oh, me, I guess.
>
> She: You know that stuff won't come off. It's permanent.
>
> Me: It's my car!
>
> She: Is it? You seem sorta young.
>
> Me: What? Do you think I stole it?
>
> She: This car doesn't really seem like you—that's all.
>
> Me: Well, it's me. This car is definitely me. Would I write on the dashboard if I had stolen it?
>
> She: I would.

Silence. Conversation. Silence. Conversation. She notices a million things.
She notices the writing on the dashboard even before I notice it myself: *One straight shot.*

I wrote it this morning, but I forgot.
These things just rise to the surface, you know.

I-70 West: Mile Marker 18

✳ 270 Miles to Zanesville

I remember sitting on Stanley's lap
as we mowed circles and zigzags into the yard—
me at the wheel, Mom laughing.
Stanley's breath like smoke and beer.
My father had only one rule:
no one was to touch the 1969 Plymouth Barracuda,
which he kept in the heated garage
under a tarp, and which he never drove.

Grandpa says Stanley bought the car
with the last of my mother's life savings.
Mom said Stanley bought it as an investment
and she kept it around for the same reason.
See that car, Zane? That's your college fund, honey!

Zach says one day Mom got in the car,
rolled down the windows,
and started 'er up with the garage door down.
Stanley was outside mowing on the Toro,
so he couldn't hear the Cuda's rumble.

Mom botched the suicide.
And that's the last we ever saw of Stanley.

Grandpa: I shot that lazy Indian. I buried his
pot-smoking ass in the sandbox!

I was maybe four or five.
I used to dig and dig and dig—
but I never found a trace of him.

She: That's too bad.

Me: What?

She: These door locks. They're all electric.

Me: I like 'em.

She: Once you start dating, you'll know what I mean.

Me: I date. I've had plenty dates, I guess. Whatever. Nobody really goes out on a *date*.

She: What do you mean, nobody dates?

Me: You just hang out.

She: Yeah, right. Well, call it what you will, it's just too bad about the electric locks.

Me: What do electric locks have to do with dating?

She: Nothing. That's my point. A boy opens a car door for a girl and helps her get in. Then, while—

Me: Isn't that sexist? Opening a girl's door?

She: No. That's just polite. Now listen. So the boy helps the girl into the car. Then while the boy walks around to his side, the girl slides over to unlock his door. That means she likes him and she's been able to slide a little closer without looking eager. With these electric locks, all the girl does is push a button and stay put. It's all *click, click, click* and everybody sits down. Where's the romance in that?

41

Me: If you like a guy, can't you just slide over next
     to 'im?

She: How many dates did you say you'd been on?

Me: I told you. I don't date!

She: Well, I can see why. With locks like these.

It was sophomore year and time
for the Arkham Asylum homecoming dance.
I started taking Comatosasine, a miracle drug
that transforms frisky teenagers into yawning zombies.
But the choice was be a zombie or force your date
to look on in horror as you black out, drool,
chew your tongue, and begin to vibrate
like you just grabbed hold of a high-voltage wire.
After my seizure in lunch the year before,
Kitty and Calliope were the only ones
who didn't treat me like a mutant werewolf.

All I could do was write on my walls and sleep.

Kitty: You're a decent guy, Zane. You should get
           yourself a girlfriend.
Calliope: *You* don't have a girlfriend, Kitty.
Kitty: I don't *need* a girlfriend, Calliope. Zane
           needs a girlfriend. Zane knows where I'm
           coming from, don't you, Zane?
Me: No, I *don't* know where you're coming from.
Calliope: Where exactly *do* you come from, Kitty?
Kitty: I'm a spy in the house o' love, baby. I know
           all about this shit.
Calliope: Oh, brother.

Kitty: It's all about Mars and Venus. Zane knows what I'm talkin' about.

Me: Kitty, I never have any idea what you're talking about.

Kitty: Well, that's why you don't have a girlfriend.

Me: That, and the seizure thing. Oh, and the suicidal mother thing.

Calliope: Actually, Zane, most girls I know think you're cute and funny and a very talented artist. You just have too many issues.

Me: Too many issues? Should I reduce my personality from weekly to bimonthly or what?

I-70 West: Mile Marker 3
255 Miles to Zanesville

Libba examines a map in her lap.
She removes her shoes, rests her feet on the dash.
They are girl feet:

                       they've been tended to. Smooth,
olive skinned. Toenails painted pink.
I want to trace around them with a marker
to prove to myself that they are real, to keep
their outline on the dash as evidence—
a snapshot for the suicide scrapbook.

She: Are you sure you know where you're going?

Me: Yes. I planned it all out. Interstate 70 goes
directly there. One straight shot.

She: Well, it's not as straight a shot as you think.
I-70 turns north up ahead, and it goes way up
through Pittsburgh. But you can take I-68
straight on and then hop on I-79 in
Morgantown. I-79 reconnects with I-70 and
you'll miss Pittsburgh altogether. I don't think
I'd drive through Pittsburgh in a stolen car.

Me: It's not stolen, for Christ's sake!

She: Please don't use that expression. It's disrespect-
ful. You just might need a savior one day.

Me: Oh yeah. I could sure use a savior now. What
would Jesus do if he were in *my* shoes?

She: He would take I-68 instead of I-70. That's what Jesus would do.

Me: Will you *please* take your feet off the dash?

She: This is our exit, just ahead.

I take it.

✱ 246 Miles to Zanesville

She: Funny.

Me: What's funny?

She: This is such a great car and all, but they didn't think to put in air-conditioning.

Me: Air-conditioning? With this much engine under the hood, there's no *room* for air-conditioning!

She: You mean this car is not built for comfort; it's built for speed.

Me: Exactly. That's the Barracuda. She's built for speed.

She: Why *she*? Why do cars always have to be females?

Me: I don't know. Why not? It doesn't mean anything.

She: No. It means everything. You call a car *she* because it's something you possess.

Me: What? I suppose if I called her an *it*, you'd think I was insensitive.

She: No, I'd think you were sensible. Anything is better than *Barracuda*.

Me: What's wrong with *Barracuda*?

She: *Barracuda* is a derogatory term for a woman who sleeps around.

Me: I never heard that.

She: Well, it's true, and I don't appreciate it. Why is it that if a girl sleeps around, she's a barracuda but if a boy sleeps around he's a stud? My father is like that. The king of the double standard. Boys can run around with every girl in sight. But girls are supposed to stay at home and keep their legs crossed until they've got a ring on their finger. Is your father like that?

Me: My father isn't like anything. Can we talk about something else?

She: I didn't bring up the Barracuda thing. That was you.

Me: Look, there's no AC. Roll down the window if you want. There's no AC. And *please* take your feet off the dash!

She: It's just funny—that's all. And can you *please* pull over at this rest area? I need to tinkle.

I-68 West: Rest Area
✳ 242 Miles to Zanesville

Waiting for Libba in the car,
the sun soon puts me to sleep.
I begin dreaming at once.
There I am on a sunny day,
four years old, digging in the sandbox
with my hands. Digging like a dog,
laughing and having fun.
Mom sits across the yard
in a lounge chair. She wears
a swimsuit, wide-brimmed sun hat,
and she's laughing at my antics.

I've dug down maybe ten inches,
deeper than I've ever been,
when my fingers slide against
something soft—flesh, eyes, a nose,
dark hair. And there, staring up at me
is a man's face. My father's face.

I scream
            myself awake and look to see
if anyone has heard. Libba's in the restroom.
The parking lot's empty except for one man
who sits on a picnic bench. He wasn't there
before. No other car but mine. The man

watches me. A man I know: Broad face. Barrel chest. Jet-black hair. I walk over to the stranger.

Me: Dad?

Stanley: Sit down, son. We need to talk.

You're looking good, Zane. You must be cutting the grass all by yourself now, eh? And driving the Cuda too, I see. You've really grown up.

No thanks to you.

Ah, you're upset. You're mad. Well, of course you are. I intended to come back. Honest. I decided to check into a rehab program the next day. So I figured I'd have a few drinks to celebrate. One final good-bye bash. I hadn't counted on dropping dead like that. That death thing came out of nowhere.

Grandpa says he shot you and buried you in the sandbox.

Well, Earl would say something like that, wouldn't he?

Is it true? Did he shoot you?

He shot *at* me. But he missed. He *did* ruin a perfectly good lawn mower, though. He used the old flintlock pistol.

The Fool's Fire-Hand.

Yes. The Fool's Fire-Hand. Actually, it's the pistol that I need to talk to you about. I need to tell you the gun's history.

Zach says it was used to kill white people during the Revolution.

Well, that is true. But there's more to the story. You see, a British officer gave the gun to a distant relative of mine (of *ours*) named Bear Breaks the Branch.

Bear Breaks the Branch?

Yes. The officer gave it to him as a gift. At the time the Wyandot, the Shawnee, and many other nations had joined forces with England. Their target was Fort Henry in the crook of Wheeling Creek, by the Ohio River. The local Indians called the area *Weelunk,* the place of the skulls. Bear Breaks the Branch was a warrior respected among his people. Here's the story:

There are just over four hundred Indians and a handful of British soldiers against not even a hundred whites inside Fort Henry. But the whites are dug in. Steep bluffs protect the fort on two sides. The other two sides are protected by a sturdy cabin that sits not forty yards from Fort Henry's southwest corner. A handful of whites are in this cabin. Any Indians who cross the open ground approaching the fort are caught in the crossfire. Twice during the night our people rush the fort, only to be repelled.

The Indians decide to burn the cabin down. Late in the night Bear Breaks the Branch crawls along the ground, undetected, with a smoldering torch. Then he stands and begins to wave the torch about to bring its flame to life.

Without warning, the cabin's window shutters fly open. A black man, rifle in hand, is there and momentarily freezes with a start. The man, a slave they call Daddy Sam, has been taken by surprise. Both men move at once to draw their guns. Bear Breaks the Branch is able to raise his prized pistol more quickly than Daddy Sam can lift his own cumbersome musket. The warrior squeezes the trigger. The pistol misfires. Daddy Sam shoots, and the Indian falls as if dead. But the bullet has only grazed the warrior's skull. Bear Breaks the Branch is left unconscious but very much alive.

Morning comes. The fort is quiet. Many Indians are just beginning to wake up. A small door opens on the fort's southern side. Out comes a young white woman who walks down the slope toward the blockhouse. She is about your age. Her name is Betty Zane.

The chiefs call out, "Squaw, squaw!" and tell the others to hold their fire. The warriors all jeer and laugh. There would be no honor in cutting the woman down.

She moves casually as if walking on an errand. The Indians watch. The blockhouse door opens to receive her. The braves joke that the woman must be searching for her husband.

After a short time Betty Zane reappears at the cabin door clutching a bundle in her hands. Gunpowder! Suddenly this is no joke. The chiefs all yell out, "Shoot now! They've run out of gunpowder. Stop the girl and the fort is ours! She must not reach the fort!"

And so our ancestors fire. A rain of bullets falls. But the Zane girl is protected by spirits. No bullet touches her. The sound of gunfire, though, has roused Bear Breaks the Branch. Still groggy, he rolls onto his side and finds the pistol. He confirms that it's still loaded and looks to his priming, making sure this time the gun will fire. He shoots the pistol just as the young girl reaches the fort's gate.

But, as I say, Betty Zane has strong medicine. Plus she is agile. As she dives for the gate, the bullet of Bear Breaks the Branch tears through her petticoat and lodges harmlessly into the door frame.

With their powder restored, the defenders of Fort Henry will be able to hold out long enough for white reinforcements to arrive. The Wyandots value their lives too dearly. The tiny fort is not worth the risk. It seems that young Betty Zane has saved the day for the whites.

Bear Breaks the Branch is not pleased. He claims evil spirits control the gun. He spends hours reenacting the event, placing petticoats on trees and shooting at them from his belly in the dirt. The others laugh at him and call him a fool.

And so the gun comes to be called Fool's Fire-Hand. It is passed on to any person in the family in danger of making a foolish choice. Whoever possesses the gun may ask the spirits within it for guidance or the answer to a question. You pray over it and the answers will come. Or so the superstition goes. The gun has been given to many of our ancestors over the years. Once the spirits pass on their wisdom, the gun goes to the next "fool" in need of clarity.

And so how did you end up with it?

Oh, I came by it honestly! Ha, ha. I made a lot of foolish moves in my day. My own mother gave it to me because she felt I was ruining my life.

What did you do?

What foolish thing did I *not* do? I drank. I drank a lot. I threw away many opportunities. Worst of all, I loved your mother. And then I married her.

What was so foolish about that?

Nothing. It was only my mother who thought so. She knew how much your grandfather hated me. But it was more than that. My mother felt that I was turning my back on my ancestry. Not only was I marrying a white woman, I was marrying a white woman who was also black! Ha! That nearly killed her.

Why didn't you take the gun with you when you left?

That was not a conscious choice. Thanks to your grandfather, I had to leave town suddenly. And then I died, of course. Not much I could do after that. You might say that I passed the gun on to your mother, even if by accident.

Fat lot of good it did her.

Well, after all, it is just an old superstition. The important question now is, What are *you* going to do with it? It seems as though the Fool's Fire-Hand has passed to you.

I-68 West: Rest Area

Now I'm standing alone next to the bench
where my father had been. A cold wind blows
over the empty picnic grounds. Rain coming.

Our ancestors, he had said. *Our people.*
Branches to add to the family stump.
My people. I think about my mother
asleep in Zanesville with Grandma Katie.
I don't notice Libba approach, nearly
jump out of my skin. My Indian skin.

    She: There you are!
    Me: Uh, hey.
    She: What're you doing over here, Zane?
           Contemplating life?

I-68 West: Mile Marker 52
✷ 226 Miles to Zanesville

Libba stops talking to write in her notebook.
She's slouched in her seat, feet out the window,
ten painted toenails in the wind, curling,
uncurling, curling. Uncurling. Slowly.
I flip through radio stations listening
for something good, but Betsy Cuda has
only AM, so it's mostly static.

Libba finds an oldies station: Bob Dylan.
The Beatles. Joan Baez. The Beatles.
Mary Travers. The Beatles. Finally
I've had enough and switch the dial to news.

*. . . good news for bird-watchers. The elusive ivory-billed
woodpecker, long considered extinct, has been sighted in the
inaccessible forest swamps of eastern Arkansas. For more
on the story, we go . . .*

Libba looks up from her writing to listen.
The story wraps up. She claps. Grabs my arm.

> She: Did you hear that?
> Me: Yeah, so what?
> She: So what? So, it's a miracle!
> Me: I was thinking it was maybe just a slow day for
>   news.

She: Maybe you should spend less time watching cars and more time watching birds. Look, it's right here in my Peterson guide.

She reaches into her bag and takes out the small bird book. She points to a drawing that looks to me like a pterodactyl.

She: The ivory-billed woodpecker, see? Similar to the pileated, but it's not. It's got the extra wing bars. And it's slightly larger. Look there, written under the picture: EXTINCT. But it's not! Many Native Americans believed the bird had magical powers. I wonder how far we are from Arkansas.

Me: You'd go to a swamp in Arkansas just to see a bird?

She: Yes, I would. It's such a message of hope. It's wonderful, like Rip van Winkle. The mysterious Rip van Winkle bird finally wakes up and wants to be seen.

Me: Maybe it wants to be left alone.

She: It's not just about the bird; it's about everything. It's the Rip van Winkle bird. It once was extinct, but now it's back. It's like falling off a cliff, but someone catches you by the collar at the last second and hauls you back in.

Libba opens her notebook. Starts to write.
Radio goes to static. I watch the road.
I think about Mom and the old man.
And every so often, I check the sky.

I-68 West: Mile Marker 49

I guess my grandfather was about
the meanest person I know. He never
hit me or Zach or Mom, but I wonder
if maybe a hard slap would have been better
than the lack of love.

                    If you really want
to hurt a kid, just don't love 'im.
And if you want to hurt 'im worse, don't love
his mother either. How could he not love Mom?

I could hear the old man in the kitchen at night.
He would say her name like it was something filthy.
Ee. Liz. A. Beth. He would beat her with it.
He would beat her with her own name.
Ee. Liz. A. Beth. This. Ee. Liz. A. Beth. That.

Every day. Every holiday. Every birthday.
When she was happy. When she was sad.
When she lost a job or found a job. When
she got her GED. When she got sick.
When she was in the hospital. Always.
Ee. Liz. A. Beth.
               Ee. Liz. A. Beth.

And I couldn't do a thing about it
but write on my walls and try not to think.
And all that came out was nonsense.

We eat the organs of cute little bunnies.

Permanent. Permanent. The ink would seep in.

She: Listen closely for the clues.
       All the answers are right in the riddle.

Elizabeth, Elspeth, Betsy, and Bess,
They all went together to seek a bird's nest.
They found a bird's nest with five eggs in;
They all took one and left four in.

Me: But what's the question?
       It doesn't really ask a question.

She: There is no question. It's just a situation.
       You've got to guess the situation.

Elizabeth, Elspeth, Betsy, and Bess,
They all went together to seek a bird's nest.
They found a bird's nest with five eggs in;
They all took one and left four in.

Me: Four girls found five eggs and left four.
She: But they ALL took one.
Me: So they all took *one* egg.
She: How can four people carry one egg?
Me: I don't know. It's your riddle.

She: You're not trying to think out of the box!
Elizabeth, Elspeth, Betsy, and Bess.
Those are all names for Elizabeth.

Me: Okay, so they're all named Elizabeth?

She: No. No. No. They are *all* just one girl!
I think it's clever.

Me: It would be more clever if it answered a question.

We went on that way for miles.

Me: Is that a diary?

She: It's my journal. A place for my thoughts. Ideas. New words I've discovered. I write in it every day. I observe the world. It helps me stay sharp. I'm going to be a poet. Or an actress who writes poetry. So I try to write a little bit every day.

Me: Like a diary. You write about love and stuff?

She: No. Girls write in diaries about love. Poets write in journals about holding hands. See what I mean?

Me: Uh. Yes, I see.

She: No, you don't. I can tell.

Me: It doesn't really matter. I was just trying to make conver—

She: Most people observe the world as if they are in the passenger seat of a fast-moving car. Poets, in contrast, view their world as if they are pedestrians walking along the roadside. From the car, travelers see the grass as a green blur. Walking along the road's shoulder, the grass becomes individual blades. And the blades are more than just green. They are twenty *shades* of green. And some are brown. And on the tallest blade of grass, a beetle is reaching upward, as if trying to touch the sun.

Me: That's cool. I guess.

She: There are all these poems out there just waiting to be written. Just look out the window and there they are! You can see them everywhere.

Me: I can see a McDonald's. Are you hungry? They take credit cards now.

She: No.

Me: Sure?

She: I'll have a coffee. And a hamburger. No, a cheeseburger. And French fries. And ketchup. And one of those apple pies. With the stripes.

McDonald's Drive-Through
Cumberland, Maryland

Drive around to the first window, please.

Speaking into the drive-through intercom,
I order Happy Meals for both of us,
then I drive the Cuda to the first window.
In the place where the drive-through attendant
should be stands instead a no-shit Indian
wearing nothing but a loincloth, his brown
chest and wrinkled face painted with colorful
shapes and symbols. In his hand he holds
the decapitated head of a bird,
and he stares at me in defiance.
Then he speaks in a strange language,
but somehow I understand every word.

> He: Welcome, Zane Guesswind. I am Bear Breaks the
>   Branch. That will be six dollars and fifty-one
>   cents.

I do not have long, Zane Guesswind. You are now keeper of the Fool's Fire-Hand, and you are facing a deadly decision.

No, I'm not facing a decision. I've already made up my mind. I'm going to Zanesville to join my mother forever. There's nothing to decide.

So, join her forever. What do I care? But hear me out. You may have another choice.

What are you talking about?

You can bring her back to life. With this. It is a magic calabash.

It looks like a bird's head.

It is a sacred bird with many powers—the bird you call the ivory-billed woodpecker. It began its journey far to the south and passed through many hands before it found its way to me. I traded a pistol for it. The brother of the pistol you now have.

What makes a moldy bird's head so special?

It has been made into a sheath to cover a small gourd within it—the magic calabash.

Calabash?

Yes. It is a vessel to collect the souls of lost loved ones. Once you have reached the land of the dead.

How does it work?

Simple. Sneak up on your mother's soul and place it in this vessel. Stopper it tight, so it will not escape. You may then return it to your mother's body. But first you must find her soul.

And where will I find my mother's soul?

Ha, ha. You will find the soul where all souls are found. In the land of the dead.

And how am I supposed to get there?

You have the Fool's Fire-Hand? Is this true?

Yes.

Ha, ha. Well then, Zane Guesswind, descendant of Betty Zane, descendant of Daddy Sam, descendant of Bear Breaks the Branch. Use it.

McDonald's Drive-Through
Cumberland, Maryland

> Me: What do you mean, descendant of Betty Zane
> and Daddy Sam?

The Indian is smiling now and reaching out
to hand me the ivory-bill's head. I can see
the neck of the gourd sticking out
from the bird's open beak.

> He: Go on. Take it.

I could capture her spirit.
I could bring her back.

Would you like a different one, sir?

The Indian is gone, replaced
by the drive-through attendant,
an annoyed teenager who rolls his eyes.
He's holding the moldy bird-head calabash,
only now it's wrapped in plastic.

Look, sir, do you want the toy or not?

No, it's not a bird's head at all.
It's not a magic calabash.

It's just a plastic Happy Meal toy
in a plastic Happy Meal wrapper.

I grab the toy and throw it in the back.

> Me: This one's fine. And thanks for nothing!

Now Libba is staring at me.

> She: Are you okay?
> Me: Yes, yes, yes. I am A-okay.
> She: You're acting a little weird.
> Me: Well, what isn't weird?

Excuse me, sir?

Now the kid at the window is speaking to me.

Is something wrong?

> Me: What did you mean about Betty Zane and
> Daddy Sam?

Sir, I don't know who—

> Me: You goddamned mighty Indian warrior.
> Coward! Go on back to your tepee and practice
> shooting petticoats.

And I drive away from the window,
the frightened kid watching me go,
rolling his eyes, looking after me
like I'm a nutcase, which, the whole
world knows by now,

I am.

She: "We eat the organs of cute little bunnies." Oh, that's pretty good. Now my turn. Hmmm. Okay, read that one.

We have finished our Happy Meals.

Me: "Kilroy was here!" Nice. That one is a classic.

Libba has convinced me to park the car and rest.
We sit in Betsy Cuda in the McDonald's lot,
each of us taking a turn writing on the dashboard,
then reading aloud what the other has written.

She: "The old man's long gray ash." Weird.
Me: "Love is the answer"? Oh please. Here's one for
    you. "Why are you going to Zanesville?"
She stops to think.
Then she looks me in the eye.

She: An albatross.
Me: Do what?
She: You know. An albatross. It's a huge seabird that
    can fly nearly forever. In the poem "The Rime of
    the Ancient Mariner" this sailor kills it and he's
    forced to wear it around his neck for all

eternity. It drives him insane. That's his punishment, to wear this dead bird around his neck and tell his story to whoever needs to hear it.

Me: So you're going to Zanesville to get an albatross?

She: Well, no. Actually, if you must know, I'm going to visit a grave.

Me: You're going to Zanesville to visit a grave? What grave?

She: The same grave you're headed for. Seems to me you need looking after. And I know Zanesville like the back of my hand. I was born there. Zanesville is where my parents met. Momma's car broke down on her way through. Daddy rescued her. They got married a couple weeks later. Isn't that romantic?

Me: If you say so.

She: Well, it is.

Me: I wouldn't know much about happily married parents.

She: Well, believe me, my folks are not Ozzie and Harriet Nelson. My father is pretty bitter. And my mother is—. She was—. Let's just say she wasn't very truthful. She left Daddy when I was ten. She picked me up from school in a taxi. When we got to the house, she handed me some old family photos, and she kissed me on the cheek. Then she rode off in the cab and never came back.

Me: My father did that. Stanley. He walked out when I was four.

She: I'm sorry.

Me: So that's why you're walking to Zanesville,
          Ohio—to visit family?

She: It's a family reunion. Ha.

Me: But why walk?

She: Why drive a stolen car?

Me: I'm telling you for the last time. This car is
          mine.

She: If you say so.

Like I said. A last-word girl.
She digs through her McDonald's bag.
Finds a French fry.

She: Ha, ha! My lucky day. And I thought I had eaten
          you all.

I-68 West: Mile Marker 34

The Golden Arches are ten miles behind
when my stomach begins to squeeze and turn.
Our Sharpie session has left the Cuda's
dashboard pretty much covered with scrawl.
Fat raindrops splat like gunshots. Then heaven
pours down. So I set the windshield wipers
on high and slow the Barracuda to a crawl.
Libba, unfazed, puts away her bird book
and reads aloud another dashboard phrase.

> She: "Zane, Zane, Weather Vane. Mommy went insane."?
>
> Me: That's what the kids in school used to chant. My mom kind of went nuts.
>
> She: You mean she was mentally ill.
>
> Me: Actually, yes. Schizophrenia. Grandpa said it started when she was a teenager. They say it got worse after she married my father. Just before my brother was born. She first tried to kill herself when I was four. I don't remember that first time very well. To me she was always really up and happy. Really optimistic and fun. But then she sorta went downhill—no thanks to my grandfather. He always acted annoyed with her, as if she had *chosen* to be sick. Eventually she got it right, though. The suicide, I mean.

She: That's heavy. You should really write about all
        that. That's what I do. In my journals. It really
        helps me to deal.

Me: I write on my walls. Weird, huh?

She: Makes sense to me. Your walls (and your
        dashboard)—they're your own version of a
        journal. But why write "Zane, Zane, Weather
        Vane"? Why write down words that some jerks
        made up to torment you? Why not transform
        the words and make them your own? After all,
        it's your name. It belongs to you. When I was a
        little girl, the other kids would change my
        name into something bad.

Me: How did they change it?

She: Don't ask. Just trust me. So I renamed myself
        Libba Ration. Hello, sir. My name is Libba. But
        you may call me Libba Ration! Get it?
        Liberation?

Me: How would you transform a name like Zane?

She: Let's see.

She uncaps a Sharpie. Then she proceeds
to alter the words on the dashboard. Sighs.
Satisfied. Begins to tap out a beat.

I-68 West: Mile Marker 32

* 206 Miles to Zanesville

She: *Zane, Zane, Weather Vane.*
        Golden sun and pouring rain.
        Round the world and back again.
        Zane, Zane, Weather Vane.
        Golden sun and pouring . . .

And she repeats it over and over
while I tap along on the steering wheel.
We try it as a round, wipers keeping
steady rhythm. We laugh until it hurts.

She: You know, Zane, you can't let events control
        you. It's okay to remember things if you must,
        but don't let their memory control you. You
        seem like a nice guy. I don't know what you're
        running from or why you flinch whenever a cop
        drives past—I won't even ask. It's just really
        good to hear you laugh. Admit it. Doesn't it feel
        good to laugh a little?
Me: Yes, Libba Ration. It does.
She: I mean it's not as if you've *killed* anyone.

The old man is suddenly back in my mind,
sitting on his La-Z-Boy in front of *Wheel of Fortune:*
sightless eyes, oxygen tubes, long gray ash.
The blotch of ink where his name used to be,

where in anger I had erased him from the light.
The smudge on the trunk of the family tree.

My stomach twists and lurches. I ease up the gas
and pull Betsy Cuda to the shoulder.
Step into the rain. Shut the door behind me.
My temples pound. The water falls in sheets.
Drenched to the skin, I fold over, crying,
my hands on my knees. And try as I might,
I cannot keep the Happy Meal down.

I-68 West: Mile Marker 30

Kitty, who was a year ahead of me,
dropped out of school during sophomore year,
which meant I had to ride the bus.

Bus number L7.

The same bus I rode when I was little.
Back when Mom would be waiting for me
at the bus stop after school. And as soon
as I stepped off, we said our routine greeting:

> She: There's my main man!
> Me: There's my main mom!
> She: How was your day?
> Me: It was A-okay!

Then we'd walk to the house for a glass
of milk and a PBJ on my favorite plate.

But by the time I was in tenth grade
Mom had long since stopped meeting me.
She rarely left the house at all. She tried
to act busy, but she mostly just cried.

By then I was doing all the cooking,
and cleaning up the house, and tending Grandpa—

anything to give my mother the space
she needed to pull herself together.

Mom stopped going to work. I bought groceries
and cigarettes using cash the old man
handed me from the stash in his closet.
He always slipped me an extra twenty.

I didn't tell Zach how bad Mom was 'cause
I figured he would commit her again.
Then one day while I was sleeping in school
and Grandpa was sleeping in the La-Z-Boy,
my mom made me a PBJ and poured
me a glass of milk (for when I came home).

She gathered a few of her favorite things.
Then she went out to the garage,
climbed into the passenger side
of the 1969 Plymouth Barracuda—
    black-tape accents,
    440, midnight blue.
She shut the door,
rolled up every window,
pushed down every lock—
    twin dummy hood scoops—

positioned my father's flintlock
pistol under her chin,

and pulled the trigger.

I-68 West: Mile Marker 29
* 203 Miles to Zanesville

I keep the Cuda's headlights on,
the rain so thick, the clouds so dark,
it may as well be night. With a yawn
Libba pulls out a blanket, curls up,
and, without a word, falls fast asleep.
I stop at a gas station for coffee
and to change out of my wet clothes.
Libba never even leaves the car.

Back on the road, I glance over at her.
I examine the blanket for the first time:
thin blue flannel, somewhat worn,
and stamped with faded black letters:
Property of Montgomery County Hospital.
Easy to read, even in the dim dashboard light.
The blanket rises and falls with each breath.

I feel like a pervert.

I focus on the road ahead:
the steaming black pavement
wet from the rain.

I-68 West: Mile Marker 24

The rain still falling. Sky still dark. The wipers
pushing aside the water. I come up behind
a big Chevy Suburban, the kind
with a television in the back for the kids.
The Suburban is dark inside except for
the bright screen. I slow down, keeping a safe
distance but close enough to make out the picture.
The movie is an old black-and-white western.
I recognize John Wayne, holding a rifle,
riding atop a stagecoach.
                              My eyes strain
   to follow the action through the darkness and rain
   and the wipers' steady *swish-slap*.
   Then John Wayne is gone, and the stagecoach is gone.
   And in their place I see Stanley on a Toro lawn mower.
      Like an old home movie. Then there I am
      posing with my mother and Zach,
      smiling and all of us in our swimsuits.
      My mother sprays us with a hose.
   Zach and I run off and then it's just Mom
   going all cheesecake for the camera,
   and she's got on sunglasses, and around
   her shoulders is the blue hospital blanket,
                        then she's not my mom but Libba
                        and she's beautiful and laughing

and my father is in the background
passing by on the riding lawn mower.
Then the lawn mower is being driven
by a man with a long, fake, white beard
like Rip van Winkle, only this time
Rip van Winkle is wearing a McDonald's cap
and twirling the ivory-bill head on a string.
He pulls down his fake beard and laughs
and it's the Indian, Bear Breaks the Branch.
But then it's me on the lawn mower
with Grandpa sitting on the back:
Ee-liz-a-beth, this. Ee-liz-a-beth, that.

Then my mom and John Wayne are on the mower.
My mother is clutching John Wayne's waist:
Thanks for saving me, Duke!
God knows my son wasn't able to do it.

I-68 West: Mile Marker 16

I place my foot on the gas
and the lawn mower's engine roars
and the Suburban's video screen veers
and I'm back in the Cuda
only two wheels on the pavement,
the other two slipping off onto the shoulder,
pulling the whole car off the road.
I'm suddenly wide awake
and jerking the wheel back toward the road.
The car fishtails and screeches
as one of the back tires blows out
with the sound of a cannon blast.
Happy Meal toys and Mountain Dew bottles
fly from the backseat to the front.
I slide in the gravel and finally muscle
the Cuda to a halt off the road.

I stop the wipers.
I cut out the motor.
Turn on the emergency flashers—
they make a little ticking sound each time they flash.

Tick tick tick tick.

Libba is still asleep under her blanket.
She slept through it all.

I think of the Rip van Winkle bird.

Then there are more lights.
Brilliant blue.
The grille of a Ford Crown Victoria
pulling up behind me.
The kind of Ford the state troopers drive.

Tick tick tick tick.

It's a cop.

"License and registration, please."

I hand the cop the license and registration
and pray they're up-to-date
and pray I look like Zachary in the dark.

"Blew a tire? I was watching.
I could tell it was a Cuda half a mile away.
Nice. At least the rain is letting up.
You won't get soaked changing it."

He looks down as he talks.
He holds a flashlight on the license
and reads it—slowly. Like it's a math problem.

"Okay, Mr.—is it Guess Wind?"
    I must have answered *Yes*.
"Okay, Mr. Guesswind, feel free to start changing your tire.
I'm just gonna run your tags and then you can be on your
    way.
Your inspection sticker is expired.
Since you're from outta state I'll let that slide,
but I'll need to run a check on the tags—
just to be sure the vehicle's not stolen. Ha."

The Ford Crown Victoria
(a favorite among law enforcement)
has a 4.6-liter motor.
Normally, Betsy could smoke a Crown Vic.
But not on a dark, wet, unfamiliar road
with only three tires and a wheel rim.
While the trooper takes Zach's license to the cruiser
I stand at the back of the Cuda, thinking.
Even though each new escape plan
seems dumber than the one before,
they all begin with changing the tire,
so I unlock the trunk and get to work.

Jack. Speed wrench. Spare tire. And—
lying beside an old toolbox, peeking
from beneath a piece of canvas—
the muzzle of the gun.

I-68 West: Mile Marker 15
✳ 189 Miles to Zanesville

My heart beats in my chest
like a trapped bird.
I stop breathing.
The Fool's Fire-Hand.

> *I shot that lazy Indian myself*
> *and I buried him in the sandbox!*

"Got everything you need?"
The cop is right behind me, smiling,
holding out the driver's license.
    I must have answered *Yes.*
"Everything checks out, Mr. Guesswind.
I'll keep the headlights on to help you see."
    I must have said *Thank you.*
He doesn't look into the trunk.
He returns to his cruiser,
the lights of which illuminate my every shaky move.
It seems to take forever to change that tire.

Once everything is packed up
and the trunk is shut tight,
I begin to breathe normally again.
I start Betsy Cuda. Put her in drive.
Then the cop is at the window—tapping.
I roll down the window.

"Your registration, Mr. Guesswind."

He shines his flashlight on the dash.

His lips move slightly as he reads to himself.

We eat the organs of cute little bunnies.
            One straight shot.
    Love is the answer.
            Give my mother back her mind.
                The old man's long gray ash.

He shines his flashlight on Libba's blanket.

Property of Montgomery County Hospital.

The Rip van Winkle bird never even stirs.

The trooper smiles a manly man-to-man smile.

"You have a good evening, now, and be safe."

I must have said *Good night.*

I-68 West: Mile Marker 15

✳ 189 Miles to Zanesville

The trooper drives away, lights flashing.
My hands shake as I sip my cold coffee.
For just an instant I am annoyed
that Betsy Cuda has no proper cup holder.

Built for speed, not comfort.

I put the car in drive.
Push the gas pedal down.
The engine roars . . .

but the Cuda doesn't move.

I leap from the car.
Oh, God. What now?
The right side tires, both front and back,
are hopelessly stuck in the mud.

I pause to have a small mental breakdown.

I-68 West: Mile Marker 15
✱ 189 Miles to Zanesville

The sky begins to rumble. I lean
against the Cuda and wonder what
Kitty and Calliope are doing.

Then I hear a distant jingle of chains,
of creaking wood and leather. The crack
of a whip and the clop of hooves on pavement.
A horse's nicker. A deep voice humming.
And through the dense rain fog a large shape
emerges, growing closer (and louder).
The shape forms itself into a team of four
large black horses pulling behind it a stagecoach
elaborately painted blue and red,
its body rocking on thick leather straps
as the driver tugs the horses to a stop.

The driver himself is middle-aged,
weathered, leather-faced, slow and calm.
He wears a black top hat and a gray
rain slicker that reaches his ankles.
The man ties off his reins, heaves
at a long wooden brake handle, climbs
down from the driver's box, tips his hat, and bows.

He: Mr. Guesswind?
Me: Yes?

He: Grandson of Katie Bell?

Me: Yes.

He: Name's Richard Shadburn. I was told you'd be
      needing some help. Looks like you're in deep,
      mister.

Me: Yes.

He: I'll unhitch the team. We'll pull you out in no
      time.

Me: Thanks.

Now it's raining again. Coming down in buckets.
Richard Shadburn opens the stagecoach door.
He turns and shouts.

He: This'll blow over quick. Climb in. We can wait
      out the storm inside. We need to talk before you
      get lost.

Me: I know where I'm going!

He: I'm not talking about where you're going. I'm
      talking about where you come from. Now get in,
      kid.

Richard Shadburn

You don't know me, do you?

No, I don't.

Well, I know you. You're Katie's boy. Your grand*mama* was my grand*daughter*, see? She was a Shadburn before she married your grandpa. That would make me your great-great-grandfather.

I met some Shadburns at Grandma Katie's funeral. When I was little. But you aren't—I mean you don't look—

You mean I don't look black? Well, neither did Katie, believe me. She looked like me. I used to drive stage-coaches all up and down this stretch of road from Baltimore to Zanesville. No one suspected I was colored. Not till the end.

Why pretend to be white?

Ha. In the first place, no black man was ever hired to drive a stagecoach. Freight wagons, yes. But not the coaches. Not ever. In the second place, I was hiding out from a white man in Virginia who thought he owned me. And in the third place, there was a little law called the Fugitive Slave Act.

You—you were a slave?

Zane, do you know what it means to "follow the condition of the mother"?

I guess it means if your mother is crazy, you're bound to be crazy too.

Well, in my day it meant that if your momma was a slave, you were a slave too. Do you see this whip? Look at this whip.

I see it.

A coachman's whip. Tapered at the end with a silken cracker. Meant to make noise only; not intended to actually meet the horses' flesh. The slaver's whip, on the other hand, is designed with wire braided into the tip. Meant for cutting the skin. I was never whipped myself, though many about me *were*, including my mother.

Just for me, Master had a special treatment: he called it *smoking*. He would tie my hands and hang me in the smokehouse with the hams. For hours on end. Till my lungs were nearly ruined. He said my skin needed darkening up a bit. My skin *was* very fair, my hair nearly straight, my features not unlike Master's. Indeed I'm told that the day I was born, my bright body rose from Momma's dark flesh like a full moon against a starless sky. Mistress flew into a rage and nearly smothered me with a pillow before she could be subdued.

The day before I escaped Virginia, I had a fever. I was about your age. Momma had been up most the night, pressing a cool wet cloth to my forehead. In the morning I woke up to the sound of my mother being whipped. The screams came from far away in the fields, but I knew it was her.

CRACK! *Pray, Master! CRACK! Pray, Master!* Every lash followed by a plea. What a thing, I thought, that a boy can recognize his mother's own unique scream. It was more recognizable to me than even her laughter.

CRACK! *Pray, Master! CRACK! Pray, Master!* Follow the condition of the mother. Each lash reminded me that I was born to this—forever!

Now there I was sixteen (spitting image of the man who owned me), listening to Momma take her lashes because she was last to the field that day. And I sat on my tick doing nothing. Just sat on my tick in the dark doing nothing. But I made up my mind then and there to never hear my momma scream again.

I was a house servant. That afternoon I packed Master's after-dinner pipe with gunpowder. And just before dinner I slipped away. I had a sickle blade, a change of Master's clothes, and a trace of onions—for my feet. I kept my feet well onioned to throw off the dogs.

Wait, back up. You put gunpowder in his pipe? Did you kill him?

Naw. But I did give his face a good "smoking," so that if you looked at him and me side by side, you could no longer see the family resemblance. Ha, ha.

Eventually I made it to Baltimore and began to walk along the Cumberland Road. I figured if anyone questioned me, I'd make like I was trying to catch up to my master's wagon or running some errand or other. But it began to dawn on me that no one was suspicious. No one wondered where my master was because no one thought I was a slave! In fact, dressed as I was, in Master's clothes, they thought I was a white man! I had always been told that I could pass. Now I had my proof.

I walked right by a chain of slaves—forty or so walking in pairs, all connected by one long rope. And though I'm ashamed to say it now, I refused to look any black man in the eye. The white men smiled and doffed their hats. I got a job tending horses with the June Bug line. And in just a year I ascended to the dignity of the whip and ribbons, and I donned the coachman's top hat.

One unlucky day Master was a passenger, and he recognized me. I barely escaped with my life. But I gained the aid of a sympathetic wagoner who packed me in an oyster crate and delivered me all the way to Zanesville, Ohio.

Home of the world's only Y-Bridge.

That's right. I crossed the Zanesville Y-Bridge riding in an oyster crate. That's when I first set eyes on Annie, whose job it was to receive me and help me get farther north. You see, Annie was the granddaughter of two freed slaves named Daddy Sam and Kate. They belonged to—

The Zanes.

Exactly. The battle at Fort Henry. The battle where Betty Zane made her famous gunpowder run.

An Indian, my ancestor, Bear Breaks the Branch, tried to kill her.

The Indian, yes. But the Indian missed. And before he tried to kill Betty Zane, he tried to kill Daddy Sam. But the Indian's gun didn't go off. The Zanes gave Daddy Sam and

Kate their freedom. And they lived to an old age and died right there at Wheeling. But not before having children. And because these children followed the condition of the mother, they were free children. And those free children had their own free children. And one of those free children, granddaughter to Daddy Sam and Kate, pulled me out of an oyster crate. That was my Annie.

Annie and I ran away to Cleveland and made our own life and made our own free children and grandchildren. And one of my favorites was little Katie, your grandmother. She had my sense of adventure and my light skin, too. Katie grew up, and after I died, she left Cleveland for a while. She drove away in a beat-up Model A station wagon. Down south she met your grandfather. And it's all because of that gun (the one in your trunk). It's all because that gun misfired. Had that gun not failed to fire that night, there would never have been an Annie, nor Grandma Katie neither. And no Zane Guesswind.

What ever happened to your mother? When you left her back in Virginia.

For the life of me, Zane, I don't know. It tore me up that I couldn't save her. It tore me up. But if your wagon is hanging backward over a cliff—and the horses aren't able to pull the load free—God help me, Zane, I had to cut the traces and let the wagon fall. What was I to do?

I-68 West: Mile Marker 15

The rain lets up. Richard Shadburn hitches
the horses to the Cuda's front end,
pulls the car to solid ground with ease.
And all without even waking Libba—
the Rip van Winkle bird.

      With his team back
in place, Shadburn climbs onto the stagecoach
and releases the brake.

He: It's been a pleasure. Now, listen to me, Zane. You
   take some advice from a man who knows
   how to run away: get off this interstate and
   head up the next exit you come to. That way
   you'll be following the path of the old
   Cumberland Road.

Me: Thanks.

He: You seem to know where it is you're going to.
   Maybe now you know a little bit more about
   where you're coming from.

He wheels the horses across the median
and returns in the direction he came.
I watch his back, Great-Great-Grandfather's back.

Not bothering to face me, he tips his top hat.
The jingle of chain traces lingers awhile.
Then he vanishes into the fog.

Route 40 West: Mile Marker 41
✳ 172 Miles to Zanesville

Back on the road, I take Shadburn's advice
and exit the interstate onto Route 40,
where a sign greets me:

> U.S. ROUTE 40 WEST
> WELCOME TO THE HISTORIC
> CUMBERLAND ROAD

The rain is gone, but the sky stays dark
from clouds and the first trace of dusk.
Soon the interstate is an hour behind.
Route 40 is mostly narrow, two-way traffic,
low speed limits, and small mountain towns.
Since I emptied my stomach a few miles back,
I begin to get hungry again.

> Me: Hey, Rip van Winkle. There's a McDonald's
> ahead. Want a Happy Meal?

No answer from the passenger seat.
Libba must be exhausted.
She must not have slept for days.

> Me: Hey, you. Are you dead or what?

No answer. Something doesn't feel right.
So I reach to pull the blanket back.
But I stop short when she speaks. A groggy
voice from beneath the blue fabric.

    She: I'm hungry.
    Me: Ah. It lives.
    She: Happy Meal. Must have Happy Meal. Libba
         want Happy Meal.

Do you want onions on those?
The thin voice from the drive-through intercom.

I ask the blanket:

> Me: Hey, Sleeping Beauty. Do you want onions?

The blanket answers:

> She: Yes. Absolutely.

I answer the intercom:

> Me: Yes. Absolutely.

And what to drink?

> Me: Four coffees.
> She: Must. Have. Coffee. Black coffee.

Coffees?

> Me: Yes, coffees. Four coffees, black.

You want coffee with your Happy Meals?

> Me: Yes, we want coffee with our Happy Meals. It
> makes them more happy.

Laughter, from beneath the blanket.

Fine. Four cheeseburger Happy Meals.
Four coffees, black. And an apple pie.
That'll be $12.48 at the first window.

Route 40 West: Mile Marker 20
✳ 151 Miles to Zanesville

No Indians at the drive-through window this time.
I pay with Zach's credit card and keep on driving.
Now I'm taking care not to speed through
yet another small Pennsylvania town.
Libba and I eat our Happy Meal feast,
throw the Happy Toys in the backseat:

> plastic figures of imaginary characters
> played by plastic actors in plastic plots
> all wrapped up in plastic bags.

I explain about the blown tire, the cop,
the Suburban's video screen. The gun in the trunk.
I keep the haunted stagecoach to myself.

> She: You have a gun in the trunk?
> Me: Yes. An old antique gun. From the
>   Revolutionary War.
> She: You have a gun? Stop. Pull the car over. Now!
> Me: No. Wait—
> She: I said pull over now!

I slow down and pull
into the parking lot
of a closed-down gas station,

its windows boarded up.

Libba fumbles at her door handle.

> Me: No, wait. Don't leave. I'm sorry. I should have told you before now. I promise you, you're in no danger.

Libba laughs.

> She: In danger? Are you kidding me? I want to have a *look* at it!

I stand with Libba
peering into the Cuda's open trunk.

She: Wow. It's beautiful. Can I pick it up?

Me: Sure. Just be careful where you point it. It's loaded.

She: Loaded? Isn't that dangerous?

Me: Well. Yes.

She: Show me how it works.

Me: See this piece here? That's the frizzen. It lifts up to hold the priming powder. The sparks from the steel and flint ignite this little bit of powder in the pan. Then the fire travels through that tiny hole to set off the main charge. And then . . . BANG!

One straight shot.

Me: My brother plugged that tiny hole up. But I drilled it back.

She: And you carved the Z in the handle, for Zane?

Me: No. My brother, Zach, did that.

She: And what's all this?

Me: That's stuff for cleaning the gun. These lead
           balls are the bullets. This is a bullet mold. And
           this is the powder horn.

For a moment, as Libba holds the gun,
holds the heavy weight of it,
I try to imagine how it must have felt
resting in my mother's hands.
Libba gently returns the gun to the trunk.

She: Why, Mr. Guesswind. It looks as if you are on
          your way to a duel.
Me: I guess I am.
She: Well, then. Let me know if you need a surgeon
          to stand with you and tend your wounds. Ha, ha.

Libba reaches out and touches my elbow,
a meaningless gesture that sets my arm on fire.
Then she climbs back into the passenger seat.
She turns on the radio and searches
the static of nighttime AM frequencies,
no doubt hoping for news of the ivory-billed woodpecker.

How far into the brink of extinction,
I wonder, can I go before it is too late?

I-70 West: Mile Marker 8

Speed limit seventy miles per hour!
Finally we reach Washington, Pennsylvania,
where the Cumberland Road rejoins I-70.
The Pennsylvania back roads have worn me out.
The Cuda isn't meant for tight curves and low speeds.
It feels right to hear the engine revving again.
The mile markers zip by, ticking off the distance.
It is now fully dark. Wheeling, West Virginia,
is only a few miles ahead. Time slows.
The Cuda's headlights illuminate the road
a few feet at a time. I am getting punchy.
And Libba Ration talks on and on.

> She: Here's a riddle that I bet you'll get. It even has
> a question in it, just the way you like.
>
> Me: Try me.
>
> She: *As I was going to St. Ives,*
> *I met a man with seven wives.*
> *Each wife had seven sacks;*
> *Each sack had seven cats;*
> *Each cat had seven kits.*
> *Kits, cats, sacks, and wives,*
> *How many were going to St. Ives?*
>
> Me: I've heard that one before. It's seven times
> however many things there are. No. It's more
> than that because every new cat, sack, and

wife has seven of its own. That sounds like
trigonometry to me.

She: Trigonometry? Wow. You're smarter than you
look.

Me: Thank you. I think.

She: But you're wrong. The answer is one.

Me: Huh?

She: Listen. As *I* was going to St. Ives, *I* met a man
with seven wives. Get it? It doesn't matter
who, what, or even how many he meets. In the
end *he* is the only one going to St. Ives.

Me: How do you know? Maybe the man he meets is
going to St. Ives too. Maybe they all meet up
and then continue on together. Maybe it's like
the *Canterbury Tales,* where they're all going to
the same place. Then they meet up along the
way and tell stories to pass the time.

She: Hmmm.

For a blissful minute of silence
I think I have *finally* gotten to say the last word.
Then . . .

She: I suppose you *could* see it that way. But that's
not really the answer.

I roll down the window.

Lean my head into the rushing air.

I yell out.

Half of me laughing.

Half of me screaming.

Me: Ahhhh! Ahhhh! Ahhhh! Ahhhh!
She: What?

She: Here's a good one. Why did the inch try to join the Mile Society?

Me: I don't know. Why?

She: Because he wanted to belong. Get it? Be long?

Me: Wow. That's not even remotely funny.

She: Ooh. A tough crowd. Try this one. Why did the boy poet introduce himself to the girl poet?

Me: Because he wanted to meter?

She: You've heard that one?

Me: No, it was just obvious.

She: Oh, yeah? So what did the boy poet *say* to the girl poet when they finally met?

Me: Oh, what? What did he say to her?

She: Hey, baby. Haven't we metaphor? Ha, ha. I *knew* I could make you smile. Hey, you can use that one on your next date.

Me: I don't date.

She: So you've told me. But you must have a girlfriend. You're handsome, and you've got a boss ride—even if it is stolen.

Me: I told you, it's—. Okay, maybe it *is* stolen, just a little.

She: Ha! The truth shall set you free, Zane!

Me: But I *don't* have a girlfriend.

She: No girlfriend? Really? And why not?

Me: I don't know. Maybe they don't want to risk going out with Zane, the incredible shaking boy.

She: What about Calliope?

Me: She's a girl and she's my friend. But she's definitely not my girlfriend. And what about you?

She: Oh, there is this one guy. He's Native American. Very spiritual. My father freaked when he found out. He called me a barracuda. But I'm not. I'm a good girl. I'm trying to save myself . . .

Silence.

She: I'm trying to save myself from drowning! Ha!

I-70 West: Mile Marker 2

Besides the dead mower, and the Cuda,
and the gun, Stanley Guesswind left me
one other thing: He left me lunacy.
     If Zach and Grandpa are to be believed,
     Stanley was as wacko as my mother was.

So it's sort of inevitable that my parents
passed on the "condition" to their spawn.
Though somehow it skipped my brother.
When God was giving out brains,
He handed Zachary the latest model,
the one with the Intel processor chip.
When I was born, God handed *me*
a rusty bucket of wing nuts.

But at least my mother stuck around
to help me put my inbred skills to use
and show me firsthand how a crazy person should act.
At least she stuck around. Not so Stanley.
Stanley just up and left. He mowed the lawn
and then he left and then he died.
Went to New York and died on someone's couch.

Not that I've ever needed him.
Zach and I have done just fine.
But Mom could have used a little support.

As bad as Grandpa was, at least he never
walked out on us. (We should have been so lucky.)
The old man only ever said one thing
in reference to my father. Repeatedly.

> Grandpa: I shot that lazy Indian myself. Buried his
> pot-smoking ass in the sandbox!

I guess insanity is all relative.

I-70 West: Mile Marker 1

We pass Wheeling, crossing the river
into Ohio, the journey's final state.
Libba opens her old dictionary
and reads aloud. She claims she's attempting
to read it from A to Z. She says it's training
for being a poet.

She: Oh, here's a good one: "*Sane*. From the Latin
       sanus, meaning 'healthy.' Having or showing
       sound judgment. Of sound mind."

Me: That must mean I'm sane since I hear sounds
       in my mind all the time.

She: Wow. I'm the same way. I hear sounds too.
       Voices. Creepy. If having a sound mind means
       being sane, then I'm the sanity poster child.

Me: Sometimes my head sounds like a crowded
       gymnasium during a pep rally. One voice after
       another. I have to write it all down or else my
       head will explode. Before I could write, when I
       was really little, I couldn't release it, so I would
       black out. Even now, about five minutes before
       a seizure hits, I can hear voices—people who
       aren't there. Family members. And they're
       calling for me, like I'm a lost dog or something.

She: Well, writing is a great release for all those voices. You might be a professional writer someday.

Me: Yeah. Just as soon as they start publishing walls or dashboards. I'll be a real hit. *We eat the organs of cute little bunnies.* Even I don't know what it means. But it feels good. It feels real.

She: Aren't all words real?

Me: I guess but . . . I don't know. Just because something is real doesn't mean it's true. I'm just crazy. Like my mother.

She: Just because you're perceptive and sensitive— and slightly weird—doesn't mean you're crazy.

Me: Well, maybe I'm sane or maybe I'm crazy, but I could swear there's a cop following us.

Libba ducks under her blanket.

She: Really?

I-70 West: Mile Marker 225
✳ 72 Miles to Zanesville

It was true.

      I had been watching the cop

for the last twenty miles. He never got any closer.

He never fell any farther behind.

When I sped up, the cop sped up.

When I slowed down, the cop slowed down.

I think of the old man propped up

in the La-Z-Boy as the sun came up.

Think of Zachary finding the body.

Think how I smudged the old man from the light.

I stop thinking. Put my foot to the gas,

pulling in front of a tractor-trailer.

I stay there, hidden from view, making

the semi slow down.

          The trucker is pissed.

He lays on the horn. But I wait. I wait

until there is a steady line of cars

in the passing lane.

         Then I gun the engine,

speeding ahead while there is no safe way

for the cop to pass the truck in pursuit.

At the last second I swerve to the exit

and I race to the end of the ramp.

This is what Betsy Cuda does best,

her engine wide open, a straight stretch
of pavement.

              The cop is forced to drive on,
unable to exit because of the tractor-trailer.
I turn right off the exit ramp, tires squealing.
I turn left onto a narrow back road.
Turn right onto another.

    WELCOME TO MARTINS FERRY

I take another. And another. And another.
Until I come to the gates of an old graveyard:

     WALNUT GROVE CEMETERY
    NO ADMITTANCE AFTER DARK

Libba comes out from under her blanket.

Me: It's okay. I think I lost him.

She: Where are we? Is this the graveyard you're after? Already?

Me: No. I just got here by accident. We're still a good hour from Zanesville.

She: Oooh. Creepy. Let's have a look.

Me: But the sign says "No Admittance After Dark."

She: Exactly. This is when the spooks come out. Let's go. I bet there's a ghost just beyond the gate.

Me: But—

Libba gets out of the car.
I kill the Cuda's motor
but leave the headlamps on to light our way.
There is no one here but us.
The air is foggy and cold.
The dead are quiet in their graves.
I hear the whisper of traffic
along I-70 in the distance.

A large statue of a woman keeps watch
at the cemetery's iron gate.
It is a woman in a head scarf,

121

a blouse, and a long skirt.
She holds a bundle in her arms.

> Me: Betty Zane. At last we meet.

Libba reads the pedestal's inscription.

> She: "In memory of Elizabeth 'Betty' Zane, whose
>   heroic deed saved Fort Henry in 1782. Erected
>   by the schoolchildren of Martins Ferry, Ohio."

Libba wraps her blue blanket
around herself. She rattles the gates.

> Me: They're chained. We'd better get going.
> She: No way. We can squeeze through.
> Me: No. You . . . you're crazy.

Libba looks startled. She scowls.

> She: Crazy? Now you sound like Daddy.

I try to touch her elbow.
The way she had touched mine.

> Me: Look, I'm sorry. I—
> She: Well, you got *that* right. That's the one thing
>   you've got right.

She flinches away from my touch,
lifts the gate's padlocked chains,
and slips through the gap.
At the center of the graveyard
I think I can see a woman in a long skirt.
Just an outline. A suggestion of a woman.
Long skirts and a bonnet.
Standing in the fog.

Betty Zane has strong medicine.
Protected by spirits she is.

Me: I'm not going in there. Don't expect me to sit
        here waiting for you!
She: Drive away, then!

I get back in the Cuda and start her up.
Then I turn her off.
I lock the doors.

And I wait.

Walnut Grove Cemetery
Martins Ferry, Ohio
* 77 Miles to Zanesville

. . . and I wait.

For what seems like an hour I wait.
And I fight to stay awake.
And I lose the fight.
And my forehead falls forward
with a jarring crack
against the Cuda's steering wheel.

      Me: Ah, shit!

I'm fully conscious now
and I see Libba through the fog,
beyond the gates,
illuminated by headlights.

She's dancing.
Her arms are outstretched
and she's spinning. Her head thrown back.
Her body spinning faster and faster.
Unapologetic joy. I am lost
in the sight of her spinning.

KNOCK! KNOCK!

It's someone at the window.
I nearly jump out of my skin.
    Protected by spirits she is.
Someone at the window.
Someone at the passenger window
knocking to get in.

    She: Hello? Anybody home? Avon calling!

Libba is grinning. She is breathing hard
and glowing. I unlock the door to let her in.

    She: Sorry. I didn't mean to scare you.
    Me: I thought I saw you. Dancing just now.
    She: I was. It was great. You should try it yourself
           sometime.

Betsy Cuda rumbles to life.
                        The gravel
of the parking lot crunches under
the Plymouth's tires. We leave behind
Walnut Grove Cemetery and we drive on.

The strain of the day has sapped me of strength.
Every mile, every minute, I struggle with sleep.
We decide it's best to keep to the back roads.
We work back to Route 40, heading west,
running roughly parallel to I-70.
I keep checking the side mirrors for cops.
As a road sign flashes by, Libba reads aloud.

She: "Scenic Route 40, Historic Zane's Trace."

She does that. Reads out loud every sign we pass.
For whatever reason this doesn't annoy me.
She talks and she talks. Reads from her books,
Recites her riddles. Reads every sign.
Libba, the Rip van Winkle bird. Libba,
who had been asleep so long, helps me
to stay awake by talking. And talking.

>   She: Hey. By the way. Thanks for not leaving me back
>   there.
>   Me: Who would tend to my wounds after my duels?
>   She: I'm serious. Thanks. Thank you. You're a kind
>   person. It doesn't cost anything to be kind.
>   People forget. Kindness doesn't cost a dime.

We talk and talk. The mile markers march by.
She talks. I talk. The talk seeps into my skin.
I think of Libba dancing in the graveyard
and in my mind I dance with her awhile.

Me: . . . so after Stanley left, Zachary had to mow the lawn. After Zach moved out, the lawn mowing was up to me. Then one day I blacked out and cut across a couple lawns before I ran into a neighor's house. That was the end for me and the riding mower. I also can't drive, although I haven't blacked out in months.

She: What do you mean, you can't drive!

Me: I mean, I *can* drive, but not legally. I can't get a license.

She: You've got no license?

Me: The DMV won't give me one. Apparently suicidal, bipolar teenagers with documented histories of seizures are not allowed behind the wheel in the Old Line State. Do you want to get out?

She: No. I don't care if you have a license or not. As long as you stay on the road.

I catch myself swerving. It's nearly midnight.
I've drunk way too much Mountain Dew.
Way too much fast-food coffee. Zane's Trace
is a winding, badly lit back road.
My eyes are shot. I feel as if the car
is sitting still as the road rolls beneath it.

Me: I think I need to find a motel.

She: A motel?

Me: Don't worry. If there's only one bed, I'll sleep on
the floor.

She: You will *not*. I don't need any special
treatment. Just because we've had a few laughs
doesn't mean you need to be my knight in
shining armor. I'll just sleep in the car. In fact
I'll get my own damn room. You and your
stolen Barracuda. She's really built for speed,
isn't she? I'll bet she is. No thanks. If you've got
to stop, then stop. But I'll not be sharing a
room with some wacko kid from Baltimore
with a graffiti fetish.

Me: Okay. Whatever.

Silence.

Libba is suddenly different—cold.
It is as if we are strangers. But then,
of course, we *are* strangers. And just as suddenly,
she is back, this stranger, my friend.
Now sweet and kind. Abusing me like family.

She: I'd prefer a hotel to a motel.

Me: What's the difference?

She: Motel just sounds sleazy, that's all.

Me: I'll sleep on the floor.

She: I told you I don't need your chivalry. That's so sexist. Do you think you can just tell a few jokes, buy me a few Happy Meals, and jump into bed?

Me: I didn't say that. I told you I'd sleep on the floor.

She: Yes, but you're just saying that to be gallant 'cause you figure being gallant will get you laid. Don't disrespect me by pretending to respect me in order to disrespect me.

Me: What? Look. I don't need this. I'm going to stop at the nearest place. You can do whatever the hell you want to.

She: Oh, did you say a swear word? Heavens to Betsy! Me, oh my. You said *hell*. I heard you. I'm gonna tell. Ha, ha.

Route 40 West: Mile Marker 205

This stretch of "Historic Zane's Trace"
has more history than hotels. The nearest
little town has only one place to stay:

THE LAKE VIEW MOTEL

A PHONE IN EVERY ROOM

AMERICAN OWNED

As far as I can see,
the Lake View Motel
has neither a lake nor a view.
Though it *does* have a phone.
Local calls are a dollar each.
There is only one room available.
And the one available room

has only one bed.

The Lake View Motel, Front Office
Morristown, Ohio
✳ 44 Miles to Zanesville

No. We've got no portable cots.
Did you have a fight with your girl, or what?

I'm talking to the desk clerk of the Lake View Motel.

> Me: She's not my "girl." That's why we'd like the
> portable cot.

Well, if she's not your girl,
what's the danger in using just the one bed?
Plenty of space. It's a queen.

There are only eight rooms (A through H).
Libba is back in Room H, taking a shower.
The clerk is an elderly woman, gray hair
in a tight bun held up by tiny wooden poles
of tiny American flags that flutter
whenever she moves her head.
She wears a low-cut, frilly blouse,
a black leather miniskirt, rainbow leggings,
and combat boots.

              I had walked into
the motel's front office and found her
taking a hammer to an old television.

The TV's picture is just white snow.
Laughter and applause penetrate the static.
A game of solitaire lies on a coffee table.
The office is cluttered with birds and animals,
stuffed and mounted in natural poses.
A squirrel. A beaver. A rabbit with antlers?
An ivory-billed woodpecker in the corner.

The clerk stands up, holding the hammer.
Amazing energy for such an old woman.
Around her neck, hanging from a scarlet cord,
is a lump of lead. I recognize it at once.
It's a bullet, like the lead balls from Stanley's
Wyandot gun—the Fool's Fire-Hand.
A bullet that had been fired, misshapen
on impact. I've seen them before—when
Zach and I dug bullets from a target tree.
The old lady sees me looking and laughs.

Son, I hope to God you're lookin'
at my necklace and not my bosom,
'cause I'm old enough to be your great-granny.
In fact, I am. Only I'm much greater than great.
I'm more greats than I got time to say.

Me: No! I was looking at your bosom—I mean, your
      bullet.

Ha, ha. So you know it's a bullet, do you?
But of course you would, seein' as it came
from the very gun that's in the trunk
of that fancy automobile you're drivin'.

She tosses the hammer onto the coffee table.
She offers her hand and I take it.

Name's Elizabeth Zane, son.
But you may call me Betty.
Lord knows everyone else does.

Betty Zane

It's good you got off the interstate, boy. Zane's Trace is where you need to be right now. My brothers, Ebenezer and Jonathan, were the ones who first cut the trail all the way from Wheeling to Maysville, Kentucky, you know. They laid out the town of Zanesville along the way. Zane's Trace wasn't much more than a bridle path back then. It was wide as a horse is wide, with mud holes as deep as a horse is tall.

You don't know how good you've got it, boy. With your paved roads and your muscle car. How does that Plymouth run, anyway?

She's sweet.

Is she sweet?

Yes, ma'am. She's real sweet.

Well, I'll bet she is.

Sort of a bull on this curvy road.

I'd like to drive 'er sometime. Take 'er for a spin.

Are you allowed to?

Allowed to what?

Are you allowed to drive? When you're dead, I mean?

Hell yes, son. I can do whatever I want to now. But, I've always done things my own way. I had a hard life and then I died. So what? Oh, death has its limitations, but I'm rarely bored. Ha, ha.

I thought I saw you dancing in the graveyard, back in Martins Ferry.

Who? Me? I haven't been over to Walnut Grove in ages. They buried me there, but I never was one to linger about. Maybe it was my Miriam who you saw cuttin' a rug. Miriam was always dancing. Loved the Virginia reel. Folks called her moonstruck, crazy, but we know better, don't we, Zane?

Who's Miriam?

Miriam's my daughter. My firstborn. And I'm not ashamed of her. Though a few high and mighty Methodist biddies looked down their noses when she was born. Well, to hell with them, judging me as they did. If it weren't for me, they all would have met the Lord at Fort Henry.

When you ran for the gunpowder?

That's right, son. September 11, 1782. I was but a sixteen-year-old girl at the time. That's when I ran for the powder and brought it back to the fort. After all the shooting was over, I dug this bullet from out the fort with a knife. I had felt it tear through my clothes. I saw it splinter the wood when it hit.

I knew this was the ball that nearly killed me because it still had threads on it, from the fabric of my shift. I attached the bullet to this cord so I might wear it around my neck. And all the rest of my life, it gave me strength. It reminded me that I had done something courageous. I figured if this little piece of lead couldn't kill me, then, by God, *nothing* could! With this bullet around my neck, what I *wished* and what I *did* became the same thing.

Folks treated me like a hero for a little while, until I fell in with Van Swearingen. There I was full to the brim with what I thought was love. And there he was (with his *own* ideas about what love was). And it being a lovely summer night, and us with no chaperone . . . well. We stood beneath a big hollow tree alive with bees. And he leaned down and kissed me. And I kissed him back.

And oh how those honeybees hummed.

Then, of course, Van would not marry me, even when I started to show. I made a home for Miriam an' me, and I braced myself for a life of glances and whispers. But in the end I found that the gossip was no more the death of me than this bullet hanging 'round my neck had been.

I'm no heroine. I'm no angel. I visit the privy just like anyone else. When I brought my baby, Miriam, into this world, the good people of Fort Henry said I was disgraceful. They looked at me (with this bullet 'round my neck) and they said I was a disgrace. I found out pretty quick how heroes and lowlifes are sometimes made of the same stuff.

Bear Breaks the Branch, the Indian who tried to kill you. The one who shot that bullet. He called me "descendant of Betty Zane." What did he mean?

He meant what he said, boy. You 'n me are kin. Moonstruck or not, my Miriam grew up just fine and married a man named Zephaniah Bell. Now, Zephaniah Bell would be your granddaddy's great-granddaddy. So that's how the Zane blood passed on to you, boy.

My story is your story. I'm glad for you to find that out before you reach Zanesville. If you choose to spill your own blood, you'll be spilling mine too. And Miriam's. And your mother's. And all of our stories will just disappear like a washed-out road.

I wish I had inherited your courage.

Ha. If given a choice of dodging a bullet or stepping in its way, I'll choose dodging when I can. Anyway, to face death, you only need a dram of courage. To face life you need a good deal more.

You tell me, Zane Guesswind, which thing do you think took the most courage: Running a few feet to Fort Henry, thinking I might die? Or giving birth to my baby, knowing I would live?

The Lake View Motel, Front Office
Morristown, Ohio

* 44 Miles to Zanesville

Betty Zane picks up the hammer
and gives the television one final smack.
The picture comes into perfect view.
The sound is no longer garbled.
The show is *Wheel of Fortune*.

Baah! I've got no patience for this program.
All that spinnin' the wheel.
All that guessin' at letters to get the answer.
Give me a good huntin' dog
and a little patch of land—
I'll make my own fortune.

Then she turns off the set, walks behind
the registration desk, and disappears
into the back room.
                        Not a minute later,
she returns—the low-cut blouse, the miniskirt
and rainbow leggings, the combat boots,
American flags in her hair—only
it's not Betty Zane, and no old lady at all.

It's the young clerk who checked me in earlier,
the only desk attendant who had been there
all night. The young woman smiles at me.

Sorry, Mr. Guesswind.
I can't find that cot.
I guess whoever took it last
never brought it back.

Hanging from a scarlet choker around
the girl's neck is a tiny silver heart.
A locket. No lump of lead. No bullet.
She catches me looking, and she frowns.

Do you need a wake-up call?

    Me: No, thank you. I've had several.

The Lake View Motel, Room H
Morristown, Ohio
✳ 44 Miles to Zanesville

Back in Room H.

To be "egalitarian" (Libba's word)

we flip a coin, and Libba wins the toss.

She takes the queen. She turns off the last lamp.

I lay on the floor, a pillow under my head.

I am stretched out next to the bed.

Libba and I talk quietly in the dark.

Me: I think I ought to tell you something.

She: What's that, Mr. Guesswind?

Me: The gun. In the trunk. I was planning on using it when I got to my mom's grave. I was going to kill myself.

She: One straight shot.

Me: Yes, exactly. One straight shot.

She: You can't do it, Zane. I won't let you.

Me: No. I guess I won't. Listen to me. I've sort of reconsidered the whole thing.

She: Well, thank God for that.

Me: No. Thank *you*. It's you who made me change my mind.

She: Why me?

Me: Because you eat Happy Meals and black coffee. Because you get excited about extinct birds.

Because of your poetry and your painted toes.

Because you've been nice to me.

She: Oh, Mr. Guesswind, you're making me blush.

Me: I know it.

She: How do you know? It's pitch-dark in here. You can't see a thing.

Me: I don't need to see. I just know.

The Lake View Motel, Room H
Morristown, Ohio
* 44 Miles to Zanesville

It feels good to be out of the car,
good to be off the road, to close my eyes.
To simply be in the darkness.
My body aches and throbs.

Silence. Darkness. We both lay awake.
Each of us listening to the other one breathe.
Finally, Libba reaches over the edge of the bed
and whispers:

    She: Give me your hand.

I find her hand in the darkness
and as I hold it, my body's every ache dissolves.
My fingertips, my hand, my arm are on fire.
I can't believe the fire doesn't light the room.
Then her voice reaches down to me, like warm honey:

    She: So, Zane . . .

                    tell me about your mom.

I'm speaking on autopilot.

> Me: My mother was always kind of nuts. When I
> was really young she tried to kill herself. That
> was her *first* try. That's when my father left. I
> hardly remember any of that. Mom always
> seemed fun and happy to me. Crazy for sure,
> but she was always a good mom.

I'm tired.

> Me: A few years later, Grandpa and Zach had her
> committed after they found her burning the
> soles of her feet with sticks from the fire. She
> was in the hospital awhile. Zach had a place of
> his own by then. The old man moved into the
> house with me. Grandpa and I got along okay.
> He was pretty rough. But he meant well, I
> think. Hell, I don't know. He was such a jerk
> about my mother that I felt guilty for liking
> him. Not long after Mom came home from the
> hospital, Grandpa had the stroke. He was nasty
> as ever. And Mom kept getting worse.

I'm so tired.

Me: She wouldn't talk. Or leave the house. It was terrible. And she just faded away bit by bit until she was pretty much gone altogether. By then I was older. In high school. I had to get myself to school. I made us dinner.

I want to sleep.

Me: Toward the end it was like Mom had forgotten I was her son. Or forgotten how to be a mom. She smoked all the time. She never bathed. She smelled terrible.

I want to go to sleep.

Me: I took care of Mom *and* the old man. I didn't want to tell Zach. I didn't want them to take Mom away again. I went to school. I left her alone. I should have told Zach. Mom took the pistol out to the Cuda. And she . . .

I want to go to sleep, forever.

Me: . . . she made me a sandwich. A PBJ. She didn't say good-bye. No note or anything. I was in

school. I had left her alone. I shouldn't have left
her alone.

I'm sobbing now, like a baby.
From above, Libba runs her fingers through my hair
the way my mother used to comfort me.

The Lake View Motel, Room H
Morristown, Ohio
✳ 44 Miles to Zanesville

I want to be a kid again.

She: You're lucky you got to be with your mother as
       long as you did.

I want to be a kid again.
A little kid falling to sleep.

She: The last time I saw *my* mom, I was in the fourth
       grade. She picked me up after school in a taxi. I
       was excited about riding in a taxi. But Momma
       was in tears. She handed me a couple old
       photos and told me to keep them hidden.

Libba's voice is calm, soft.

She: The taxi stopped in front of our house. She told
       me to keep the photos in a safe place and not
       to let Daddy find them. I could see why she
       wanted me to keep them from Daddy. They
       were photos of my family. People I'd never met.
       Neither Momma nor Daddy hardly ever
       mentioned family. Momma had told me that
       she was Italian and that our relatives lived
       overseas. What did I know? I was just a kid.

I want my mother to sing me to sleep.

> She: But the faces in the photos were mostly black. Aunts.
> Uncles. Cousins. My momma's grandparents. My great-
> grandparents.
>
> Me: You mean you're . . .
>
> She: Black? That's right. At least partly. Though up until that
> time I had no idea. Does that matter?

I try to say no,
but I can no longer speak.
> Sleep sweeps over me.
> Libba's voice sounds far away.
> > Through a haze of fatigue
> > I think I hear her say my name.
> And her own name. Names of others.
Mothers. Fathers. Mothers' mothers.
Fathers' fathers . . .
> countless names like black and white sheep:
> > Elizabeth Guesswind, Katie Bell, Richard Shadburn,
> > > Betty Zane, Miriam, Bear Breaks the Branch,
> > > > Daddy Sam, Kate, Annie, Earl, Stanley,
> > > > > Zach, Zane, Libba Ration, and so many others—
> > > > all escaping reality into a world of
> > > > > whispers—
> > > > > > countless names like black and
> > > > > > white sheep

singing me to sleep.

The Lake View Motel, Room H
Morristown, Ohio
✳ 44 Miles to Zanesville

I am suddenly awake in Room H.
Awake in the dark and breaking out in a sweat.
My back is stiff from the hard floor.
I hear Libba on the bed above, crying into her pillow.

    Me: What is it?

I sit up but she isn't there.
The bed is made. Never slept in.

She isn't there.

        Then I hear the crying, from the bathroom.
        I knock. I open the door, but she isn't there.
        Then the crying is muffled.
        Someone crying in the next room,
          crying through the air duct.
Then weeping from walls on either side of me.
Walls whispering. Pennies hidden.
        I put on my shoes and walk.
        Down the hall to the snack machine.
      Behind each door I pass—weeping. Muttering.
      Mumbling. My mother sobbing.
      The old man's bitter spit. Ee-liz-a-BETH.
      Pray, Master. Ee-liz-a-BETH. *Pray, Master.*

The smell of onions, smoke, and sweat.

I begin to call out Libba's name.

No answer.

She is not there.

Only the sobbing and the sorrow.

Only the onion smell, clouding my mind.

A huge bird flies by along the corridor.

The ivory-billed woodpecker. Extinct.

The Rip van Winkle bird.

Now back in my room. Room H.

No lake. No view. One small window.

Like my bedroom. *Shaft of light in the dark.*

I call out. She is not there. Only the dark.

Smells of smoke. A fresh mown lawn.

I flip on the light and see the walls covered in scrawl.

We eat the organs of cute little bunnies.

One straight shot. Ee-Liz-A-Beth.

The old man's long gray ash.

If need be, take me instead.

Zane, Zane, Weather Vane.

Wake the Rip van Winkle bird.

Follow the condition of the mother.

And on and on and on.

How long had it all taken?

I hear gunshots and shouts somewhere outside.

Then I remember the Barracuda.

    I think of Libba sleeping there under her blanket,
    sleeping through it all.

              I reach the parking lot
and the gunshots are louder, all around me
shouts and curses, the whine of arrows in the air.

        A cannon's blast, the stink of sulfur,
        woodsmoke,
        gunpowder, blood—sleeping through it all,
        under her blanket.

                The Rip van Winkle bird.
    I grab for the handle. I open the door.
    Sleeping under her blanket.

       Property of Montgomery County Hospital.
Bear Breaks the Branch stands at the window
           raising his pistol.   *The Fool's Fire-Hand.*
Dad's pistol, aiming at Libba's blanket.
I scream, NO!

    Me: *No!* No. No.

    And I fumble my keys into the ignition.
    Betsy Cuda roars to life and I slap her in reverse,
      but the Indian is running after us, his pistol raised,
aiming at Libba. CRACK! The gun goes off.
Libba's window shatters as I crash into a dumpster.
The Cuda's engine stalls. The Indian cries out and falls.

Daddy Sam slams shut the wooden shutters.

She isn't there.

Then everything goes silent.

Then everything goes black.

The Lake View Motel, Parking Lot
Morristown, Ohio

At dawn's blush, I wake up
drooling on the steering wheel.
It takes me a moment to remember where I am.
The Cuda's front passenger door
has buckled where I hit the dumpster.
I reach for Libba and pull the blanket back

. . . but she's not there.

Just the scattered glass, Happy Meal trash,
and markers. Just the open cardboard box.
Her family photos, the toothbrush,
the Peterson bird guide, her beat-up dictionary,
her dog-eared journal full of thoughts,
and the box lid—the box lid with its label:

Elizabeth Bell Guesswind: Personal Articles

. . . but Libba is not there.

Richard Shadburn's old stagecoach rattles past.
Did I see her painted toes propped up at the window?
I shake my head. I try to clear my mind.
But Libba is not there.
I try and try and try.

Each time I open my eyes she is not there.
She has never been there.
Libba hasn't been there all along.

Route 40 West: Mile Marker 182

I've been back on the road now
for about twenty miles. The sun is up.
I want to leave the Lake View Motel
as far behind as possible.
And I need to think. I need to return
to the plan. My only comfort, my only hope,
my only way out, my little invisible
friend, has simply ceased to be.

Had I simply read my mother's journal?
Had I simply gone through all her things?

Follow the condition of the mother.

I keep to Route 40, Zane's Trace,
taking every curve slightly too wide,
driving slightly faster than I should.
No time to stop and assess
the Cuda's damage. The passenger door
will need replacing—

nothing that Zach can't handle.

Route 40 West: Mile Marker 180

Twenty miles to Zanesville.
I take a curve too fast. Veer off the road.
Overcorrect into oncoming traffic.
Back in my lane. Under control.
Coffee has spilled onto my mother's journal.
Libba Ration. The actress poet. Poet actress.
The girl who became my mother,
then became something else.
Sighted less and less on her way to extinction.
Now the old man too. Extinct.

Shit, kid! You're a worse driver than your mom.

It's the old man.
Sitting in the back.
Oxygen tubes up his nose.
Smoking a cigarette.

Eyes front, kid!
What are you tryin' to do?
Kill me twice?

> Me: Get out.
> Me: Get out of my head.
> Me: Get out of my car.

Your car? That's a bit of wishful thinking, isn't it, boy? Watch your mouth, Zane, or you'll turn out to be a liar like your grandma Katie. She said her people were Italians. Ha! What an idiot I was. She said her grandfather had raised her and all her family were dead.

Well, let me tell you something about your grandma. When she came to me she had nothin'. Nothin' but the clothes on her back and a worn-out Model A station wagon only good for scrap. Oh, crap. I was all the woman had! Earl Bell was all the woman had. Now ain't *that* a pisser?

Then little Libba was born and I did the Christian thing. Even bought Katie a ring. Libba was a smart little gal, smarter than 'er mother an' me put together. And she loved me. She made me laugh. We were doin' okay.

Then I find out that your grandma was colored, and the happy little lie unravels. The damned lying barracuda cheated me. Cheated me out of my chance for a normal life. I sure as hell wasn't gonna let her take Libba too! Maybe the little girl *was* part mongrel. But at least I knew her smile was real. Least I knew when she hugged me she meant it. I knew that I loved her and that she loved me too. Libba thought her daddy was some kind of hero.

Shut up! Shut up! Get out of my head. You're not really here.

Your mother'n me, we made do just fine. Course I couldn't even show my face 'round Zanesville because of the shame. Folks all the time whisperin' behind my back. Libba was just around ten at the time, and the kids at school were mean. You know kids. Instead of Libba Bell, they called her Libba *Black*.

And then Libba'd punch 'em in the nose! Haaaa, hoo! She was a scrappy thing. She'd fight 'em all and make 'em bleed. And o' course it was *her* that got sent home. Bastards.

When a garage went up for sale in Baltimore, you better believe I jumped at the chance. I figured on a fresh start for the girl'n me.

You treated her like shit. Why were you so mean to her?

But it all just fell apart. When Libba was a teenager, she started actin' weird. I know *all* teenagers act weird. But this was really bizarre, nutso stuff. She'd talk to herself. She started smoking. She'd wring her hands and mumble. She'd pace around the room like a penned-up dog. I sent her to a doctor, but he was no damn help. He said she had a mental condition.

Well, ain't that a pisser? Even that barracuda's *child* was defective. Oh Gawd, I loved the little girl. But the little girl kept growing up and changing. Changing into a stranger.

She got more and more crazy until there wasn't anything left for me to love. She just disappeared a little bit every day. Then she was gone. Like she was drawn out with invisible ink!

I kept asking myself where it all went wrong. I couldn't stand the sight of my own daughter! "Ee-liz-a-beth. You lost your job? Ee-liz-a-beth. Another boyfriend? Ee-liz-a-beth. You're movin' out? You're leaving me? Shacking up with some damn lazy Indian? Well, good riddance to you, Ee-liz-a-beth! Your mamma was a barracuda. Don't you be like your mamma was."

Libba was all I had. Still, I was pushing her away. An' the more my daughter made me sick, the more I made myself sick too. I was so far in it that I couldn't get out.

Maybe it was just old age. Maybe it was death creepin' up on me. But I sometimes felt like you boys were angels sent to earth by God to kick me in the ass. Especially you. "Little Z." You were like a ray of sunshine to me. Though in the end you were too little, too late.

It was not my job to fix you.

I was like a prisoner on visiting day, trying to touch my family through the shatterproof glass. I loved you boys. I never said it. I tried to show it, but by then I was too broken. The love came out all wrong. Whenever I turned the ignition, black smoke poured out the tailpipe.

I was *that* broken.

Route 40 West: Mile Marker 160
* Zanesville, Ohio

By the way, boy,
welcome to Zanesville.
You made it.

The old man takes a final pull
off his cigarette, with its crooked gray ash.
He dissolves into the air
along with his last blow of smoke.

And just like that
I arrive in Zanesville.
And in ten minutes more
I am crossing the famous Y-Bridge.
Then I'm at the center
where the three roads meet,
at the hub of a wheel that spins me,
points me in the direction of my mother.
And in ten minutes more
I'm at the cemetery.

Westbourne Cemetery,
home of Libba Guesswind's grave.
Where all of it finally
will come to an end.

Westbourne Cemetery
Zanesville, Ohio

I put the Cuda in park and leave the motor running,
I place my mother's box lid across the steering wheel
and I draw a line with a red Sharpie
through the words *Elizabeth Bell Guesswind*.
                    Above the red line I write *Libba Ration*.
I write it again.
      And again. And again.
            And when every space on the box lid is full,
            I start on the ceiling of the car
            (where all religions are written).
      I write her name end to end to end
      gradually tracing the shape of a mountain.
      And at the mountain's peak I write: LIBBA RATION!
And I draw a picture of my mother and Zach
and me . . .
            and even the old man.
I try my best to put the old man back—
back into the light.

            Then I see my own arm—smooth, white, and alive.
            I ponder it. It seems to have grown overnight.
            This living, white arm. Empty space wanting words.
And I write my name there: ZANE.
      And again: ZANE. And again. And again.
Large letters on my left forearm.
      Small letters on each finger of my left hand.

Again: ZANE. Again: ZANE.
          A letter on each knuckle: Z-A-N-E.
          On my palm. My bicep. My shoulder.
    ZANE, ZANE, ZANE. As many *Zanes*
as space will allow on my living white arm.

So when they find me here in Zanesville,
          when Zach comes to identify the body,
there will be no mistaking—

This is me.
          This is my arm.

And this is where I belong.

Westbourne Cemetery
Zanesville, Ohio

I want
more than anything
to be home, to be writing
on my walls. Harold
with his purple crayon
would have drawn a parachute,
or a big pillow to land on,
a hole to disappear into,
some clever way out.

Instead, I step out of the car.
Gravel crunches under my shoes.
I open the trunk.
I pick up the gun.

> *One straight shot.*

And I walk to the family plot.

Westbourne Cemetery
Zanesville, Ohio

The grass is still wet with morning dew
as I make my way to the far cemetery corner.
The family plot is just as I remember it.
I want my body buried here.
Next to my mother and near Grandma Katie.

I find my mother's stone easily.
It is the newest one,
the one with the brightest shine.
The one with a woman stooping in front of it.
The woman is wearing a peasant skirt.
She is barefoot. Her toes are painted pink.
Jangling bracelets encircle her wrists.
Brown chestnut braids fall down her back.

My mother.

She is arranging flowers. Daffodils.
She turns and smiles at me.

> She: There's my main man.
> Me: There's my main mom.
> She: How was your day?
> Me: It was A-okay.

Westbourne Cemetery
Zanesville, Ohio

Me: The family plot looks nice.

She: Thank you, my love. The wind blows incessantly. It sweeps up this hillside, and every leaf and candy wrapper ends up here. I try to keep it tidy. Lord knows no one else around here will do it.

Me: I'm sorry, Mom. I'm sorry I didn't come to your funeral.

She: Oh, honey. Don't give it another thought. You have other matters to worry over. I see you've brought the Fool's Fire-Hand. You must have an important decision to make.

Me: I know the story of the gun. I know about the battle at Fort Henry.

She: You've been reading my journal. Your father told me all about the gun. He knew about so many things. Your father really taught me a lot.

Me: I spoke to him a few miles back.

She: It was your father who chose to name you Zane. He knew how all the families had come together. Some coincidence. Such a coincidence has *got* to be mystical. Don't you think so, Zane? Your father thought so. You are the seventh generation. The one where all three bloodlines meet. Daddy Sam, Bear Breaks the Branch, and Betty Zane have all reunited in you. The pistol in your hand. Two hundred years ago it failed. But it's still trying. Pull that trigger today, son, and they all die. Three souls claimed by a single bullet. Go home now, Zane. Throw the gun away and go home.

Me: I can't go home. Because of Grandpa. Mom, I killed him. I did it with my walls.

She: It was not you, Zane. It was not your walls. Grandpa's death wasn't your fault. And *my* death wasn't your fault either. I know that's what you think.

Me: If I hadn't gone to school that day. If I hadn't left you alone. I could have kept it from happening.

She: No, Zane. This is not your fault. None of it is. Go back home now.

Me: Home to what?

She: You have a brother who loves you. And two good and true friends. And you have your whole history yet to live.

Me: I don't want a history. I just want *you*. I want you not to be dead. I want you not to be sick. I want Grandpa. And I want Dad. I want us all to be together. I want us all to get along and be happy.

She: It doesn't work that way, Zane. Life unravels as it's lived. It can't be woven back together.

Me: But the Indian, Bear Breaks the Branch. He said there was a calabash—a gourd wrapped in the skin of an ivory-billed woodpecker, that can capture your soul. If I go to the land of the dead, I might be able to bring you back to the land of the living.

She: Ha, ha, ha. Zane, can't you see by now that it's you? *You* are the calabash, my love. My soul lives in you. As long as you are alive, I'll be alive too.

Me: I miss you, Mom. I miss you so bad.

She: I know. I know. And every time you remember me, you pour me out. You pour me out and bring me back to life. Do you feel that, Zane? The wind is picking up again. I have to go.

Westbourne Cemetery
Zanesville, Ohio

So I drop to my knees
alone at my mother's grave
    and clasp my hands in prayer
    around the gun barrel, the muzzle
under my chin, and my finger
on the trigger.

    I pray and I pray
    to the Fool's Fire-Hand
    but no answers come.
No voices. No visions.
                No dead ancestors.
Not even the old man blowing smoke.
I may as well be praying to the dirt.
        Or the wind.
        Or the Plymouth Barracuda.
      Or a pack of Sharpie markers, never used,
        a smooth blank wall to write my nonsense on.
Or Kitty and Calliope.

    Two good and true friends.

My uptight brother with his dental floss fetish.

    A brother who loves you.

I lower the gun and stand up into the wind.
I feel like I belong here, standing in the wind.
I feel I am the wind itself.

You are the calabash, my love.

Westbourne Cemetery
Zanesville, Ohio

The sun has burned off the morning mist.
The gusting wind jostles me as I walk
back to the Cuda. That's when I see it,
there in the parking lot next to the Plymouth.
The police car is back, the one I shook last night.

I can see it better in the daylight.
Not a state trooper Ford. It's a Dodge Charger:
5.7 Hemi V8, 340 horses under the hood.
Maryland plates. A sheriff's patrol car.

Ah.

Deputy Zach has found me.

Westbourne Cemetery Parking Lot
Zanesville, Ohio

We sit in the sun
on the Barracuda's trunk.
Zach holds the gun in his lap.

Me: How'd you find me?

Zach: Where do I start? A state trooper ran the
Cuda's tags and *my* stolen driver's license. My
stolen credit card was used at Wal-Mart, the
Happy Days Diner, three gas stations, and four
different McDonald's. Oh, and again at the
Lake View Motel, where the manager claims
the walls of Room H were "vandalized with
satanic graffiti." And I also read your bedroom
walls at home.

Zane belongs in Zanesville.
Zanesville is the place for Zane.

Little brother, your movements over the past
few hours have not been difficult to trace.
When I woke up and found Grandpa, I figured
you might have come here. I thought maybe
you'd try to see Mom.

Me: I wanted to tell her about Grandpa. I think I
killed him, Zach. I killed him with the things I
wrote on my walls.

Zach: No, Zane. Grandpa was a sick old man. People
          die.

Me: I wanted to tell her that Grandpa's dead. I
          wanted to tell her I found him. He was
          watching *Wheel of Fortune*. He had a cigarette
          with a long ash. His eyes were open, Zach. The
          oxygen tubes were still up his nose. God, he
          was a real asshole wasn't he?

Zach: Yes, Zane, he was. He was a jerk-off to the
          very end.

For some reason, this last statement strikes
me as hilarious. And I laugh.
And so does Zach.

                    It feels good to laugh.
Good to laugh with my brother. I tell him
about Mom's journal, her dictionary,
her toothbrush, her blanket, her bird book, her photos.
I tell him about the ivory-billed woodpecker
come back from the dead. About the magic calabash
and the Fool's Fire-Hand. And I tell him
about my suicide scheme . . .

        One straight shot.

And Zach laughs a big brother laugh
and he assures me he had the gun "fixed."

He assures me that the gun is harmless.
Assures me the gun won't fire.
And just to prove it
he levels the barrel at my chest

and he squeezes the trigger.

Preston-Hoy Funeral Home
Baltimore, Maryland

Until the funeral I didn't think
many people knew I was alive.

Folks show up from everywhere.
Classmates from Arkham Asylum.
Cops from the sherriff's office.
A few Bells from Zanesville.
A few Shadburns from Cleveland.
Even a distant Guesswind cousin comes.
They are all there for me.
                        Me and Zach that is.
I don't think any of the guests
really cared that much for the old man himself.

This would have been a double funeral
had the Fool's Fire-Hand not misfired
that day at Westbourne Cemetery.
The wind had apparently blown
the priming from the pan
and the gun had failed, yet again,
to take the life of a Zane.
Zach fixed the gun, this time, for good,
by pouring cement down the barrel.

The old man's will requests he *not*
be buried in the family plot "as it is tainted

by Katie Shadburn's colored corpse."
So we have him cremated, per his wishes.

The funeral home gives us
Grandpa's remains in a canister
that we place in the Barracuda's trunk.
And as soon as Zach and I get home,
we bury the old man's ashes

in the sandbox.

The Guesswind Home
Baltimore, Maryland

The after-funeral party takes place
at our house in Baltimore. Zach forgets
to floss his teeth. Calliope has too much punch.
Kitty announces he is going back to school.
Zach's girlfriend, Susan, brings her brother, Wes.
Wes holds a casserole dish. I compliment
his flowered oven mitts. He tells me he's sorry
about the old man. And for a moment
we don't loathe each other.

Call it that old funeral magic.

Calliope and Kitty have brought a gift
(wrapped in black paper): a twenty-pack
of assorted Sharpie permanent markers.
So we all head downstairs to my bedroom
to write on the whispering walls.
I stand on a chair and return the old man's
name to its place in Zane-atopia.

And then he's there.

        The old man is there
holding a marker in his one good hand
and writing on the walls himself.

And next to him is Grandma Katie,
laughing and cutting up and kissing the old man's cheek.

Richard Shadburn is there. And his wife, Annie.
And Annie's grandparents—Daddy Sam and Kate.
All of them writing on the walls:
Names, dates, phrases, nonsense.
Bear Breaks the Branch sniffs at a pen.
Betty Zane traces her hand and marvels at the vivid ink.
Miriam Zane spins.

And my father is there.
Stanley is smiling at me as he writes on a wall,
and next to him, my mom. She holds out her hand
and walks me over to the sorry family tree I drew.
And all of us there—living or dead, crazy or sane,
friend or foe, black or white, family or stranger—
we all crowd around and add our own names
to the twisted, crazy-beautiful family branches.

AUTHOR'S NOTE

Zane's Trace is partly factual, partly fictional, and mostly middlin'. Baltimore and Zanesville, and every town between, are actual places. The various roads are real as well. In fact, the route Zane travels from Wheeling, West Virginia, to Zanesville, Ohio, is hundreds of years old, first blazed by the buffalo, followed by Native Americans who established what early settlers called the Mingo Trail. The Mingo Trail provided the route for Zane's Trace, which in turn became the National Road (also called the Cumberland Road or simply the Old Pike). The National Road gave way to transcontinental Route 40, connecting the Atlantic and Pacific Oceans. Finally, Route 40 has been replaced by Interstate 70.

Walnut Grove Cemetery, where Betty Zane is buried, in Martins Ferry, Ohio, is real. So is the Betty Zane statue. There is, however, no Westbourne Cemetery in Zanesville, but the incredible Y-Bridge, spanning the Muskingum and Licking rivers, is real. The bridge was first erected in 1814 and has been rebuilt five times since.

While Zane Guesswind is himself fictional, many of his "ancestors" really lived in the area through which Zane travels. Richard Shadburn was a real "pike boy"—the term used to describe any male who worked or lived on the National Road—though he was actually a wagoner, not a coachman. No one acquainted with him knew he had escaped a life of slavery. In fact, no one even knew he was black, until the day in 1842 when he was recognized

Aerial view of the Zanesville Y-Bridge (*From* the Norris Schneider Collection, courtesy of the Ohio Historical Society)

at McGruder's Wagon Yard in Pratt's Hollow by the man who "owned" him. Shadburn's "master" tried to shoot him, but the wagoner got away and was never seen again. One theory has him making a new life in Canada.

Zane's Trace, the nation's first federally funded road, was the brainchild of Ebenezer Zane, who arranged the footpath's construction through the dangerous Ohio wilderness, establishing the community of Westbourne (later named Zanesville) along the way. Ebenezer Zane and his brothers were tough customers. During the Revolutionary period, survival in the Ohio River Valley required a strength and courage that we can hardly imagine today. Around 1781, Elizabeth "Betty" Zane left her home in the safe and civilized city of Philadelphia to join her brothers near the confluence of the Ohio River and a winding creek named *Weelunk,* a Delaware Indian word meaning "place of the skull" or "of the severed head," so named because of a gruesome warning sign left atop a pole for unwelcome visitors. Thus originated the Anglicized name, Wheeling Creek, and eventually the name of the West Virginia city through which it runs.

The year of Betty Zane's birthday is contested—either 1759 or 1766. On September 11, 1782, not even a year since her arrival in this hostile frontier, Betty (sometimes called Betsy) was on hand when Fort Henry was attacked by a large force of Indians and British soldiers in what some consider the last battle of the Revolutionary War. The independent Betty really *did* make the famous gunpowder run from Ebenezer's blockhouse to save Fort Henry. Depending on what birth year you choose, Betty was either sixteen or twenty-three years of age.

Evidence indicates that less than two years later, Betty gave birth to Miriam Zane, the illegitimate child of a man named Van Swearingen, though it is unclear *which* Van Swearingen—there were a few—is the actual father. Not counting genealogical texts, *Zane's Trace* seems to be the first book to mention Betty Zane's illegitimate child in print. A perplexing omission. Surely this episode affected her life more profoundly than her heroics at Fort Henry. Van Swearingen was compelled by the court to pay Betty a sum of £100, and he later sold her a plot of land on nearby Short Creek.

Betty Zane eventually married twice. The first of her two husbands never returned from a fishing trip, presumably killed by Indians. Most sources claim she died in her sixties. She had raised eight children in all. Her first daughter, the illegitimate Miriam, really *did* marry a man named Zephaniah Bell. Zane Guesswind's grandfather, Earl Bell, however, is imaginary. Earl is named for a grumpy old next-door neighbor from my childhood. Ironically, just one house down from the real Earl lived a woman named Mrs. Bell, who was very kind and not grumpy at all.

Daddy Sam and his wife, Kate, were actual slaves owned by Ebenezer Zane. They were both present at the siege of Fort Henry, during which Daddy Sam shot an Indian who was attempting to set fire to his master's blockhouse. Once freed, they spent the last years of their lives on Zane Island, located in the middle of the Ohio River near where the battle took place. According to some, when Daddy Sam died, his gun was buried with him at his request. The children and grandchildren of Daddy Sam and Kate mentioned in this book, including Grandma Katie and Annie, are imaginary.

Bear Breaks the Branch is fictional as well, though his people, the Wyandot were—and are—very real. The Wyandot banded together with other tribes to attack white settlers (invaders?) during and after the Revolutionary War. One of Betty Zane's own brothers, Isaac, had been kidnapped and raised by the Wyandots. Isaac later married a prominent Indian "princess" and became a respected Wyandot leader who refused to join the fight against the whites. The story of the magic calabash that carries the souls of the dead comes from an actual Wyandot legend. The story of the Fool's Fire-Hand is my own fabrication. Unfortunately five of the original twelve Wyandot "clans" are now extinct. Today most Wyandot live in Kansas, Oklahoma, and Canada.

Zane Guesswind himself, along with his friends, enemies, and family, are composites—bits and pieces of folks I knew as a kid and folks I've met as a grown-up. Zane's seizures are caused

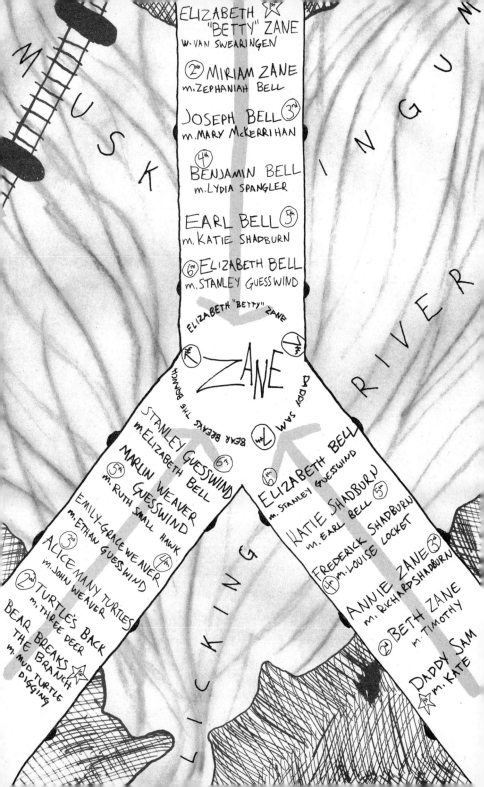

by temporal lobe epilepsy, which is also, in his case, responsible for a group of symptoms known collectively as the Geschwind syndrome (hence the name Guesswind). One of the more unusual symptoms of this syndrome is hypergraphia, the overwhelming urge to write, and write a lot. Hypergraphia has been called the Midnight Disease because those who suffer from it often stay up writing late into the night.

Like Zane, I began writing on my own bedroom walls as the result of my losing a penny behind the baseboard. So that others might know the penny was there, I grabbed a pencil and wrote, "Penny lost down here on the night of April 12, 1976, at 2 till 9 PM and 5 seconds by Allan Dean Wolf." I was thirteen. Writing on my walls became a daily activity, an expressive outlet that helped me through puberty, adolescence, and early adulthood. Like Zane I drew pictures, composed poems, scrawled nonsense, and glued objects on all four walls, my ceiling, windows, mirrors, even some furniture. My parents never gave me permission, nor did they ever stop me. Whenever I visit my childhood home in Virginia, I grab a Sharpie and walk downstairs to write on the walls. Only now, I'm joined by my three children.

Although I think muscle cars are really cool, I'm no grease monkey. I refused to let automotive reality stand in the way of a good story, meaning to say I fudged the technical aspects of some cars mentioned in *Zane's Trace*. (For example, the 1969 Plymouth Barracuda was NOT equipped with electric door locks.) I did once cover my own car's dashboard and interior with poetry and song lyrics, only it was an orange 1974 Volkswagen Beetle. Born to be wild, baby.

My author's note would not be complete without some mention of teen suicide; after all, the premise of this book is a troubled teenager's road trip to end his own life at his mother's grave. According to the U.S. Centers for Disease Control and Prevention, suicide is the third leading cause of death among fifteen- to twenty-four-year-olds. Nearly 60 percent of all suicides are committed with a gun. And teen suicide has risen by more than 200 percent since 1960.

It is a common misconception that speaking to kids about suicide will somehow make them more likely to kill themselves. Actually, the opposite is true. An open dialogue is needed. Knowledge, facts, understanding, and life itself should freely flow upon a river of talk. Check this book's bibliography for some important resources.

BIBLIOGRAPHY

Note: This is a list of the nonfiction titles I found most useful in my research. An * next to the author indicates that the book is accessible and friendly to younger readers.

ZANE FAMILY AND OHIO VALLEY FRONTIER HISTORY

Buley, R. Carlyle. *The Old Northwest Pioneer Period: 1815–1840.* 2 vols. Indianapolis: Indiana Historical Society, 1950.

Hintzen, William. *The Boarder Wars of the Upper Ohio Valley: (1769–1794) Conflicts and Resolutions.* Manchester, CT: Precision Shooting, 2001.

———. "Betty Zane, Lydia Boggs, and Molly Scott: The Gunpowder Exploits at Fort Henry." *West Virginia History,* vol. 55: pp. 95–109.

——— and Joseph Roxby. *The Heroic Age: Tales of Wheeling's Frontier Era.* Freetown, IN: William Hintzen, 2000.

Martzolff, Clemment L. "Zane's Trace." *Ohio History: The Scholarly Journal of the Ohio Historical Society,* vol. 13, no. 3 (July 1904): pp. 297–331.

Newton, J. H., et al. *History of the Pan-Handle, West Virginia.* Bowie, MD: Heritage Books, 1990.

Roxby, Joe. *Lewis Wetzel: Separating the Man from the Myth.* Manchester, CT: Precision Shooting, 1998.

*Tunis, Edwin. *Frontier Living.* Cleveland: World Publishing Company, 1961.

Withers, Alexander Scott, and Reuben Gold Thwaites. *Chronicles of Border Warfare, or a History of the Settlement by the Whites, of Northwestern Virginia, and of the Indian Wars and Massacres in that Section of the State.* Parsons, WV: McClain Printing Company, 1997.

HYPERGRAPHIA

Flaherty, Alice W. *The Midnight Disease: The Drive to Write, Writer's Block, and the Creative Brain.* Boston: Hougton Mifflin, 2004.

THE NATIONAL ROAD, TRAVEL, TRANSPORTATION

*Ammon, Richard. *Conastoga Wagons.* New York: Holiday House, 2000.

Bruce, Robert. *The National Road.* Washington, DC: National Highways Association, 1916.

*Mansir, A. Richard. *Stagecoach: The Ride of a Century*. Watertown, MA: Charlesbridge, 1999.

Searight, Thomas B. *The Old Pike*. Berryville, VA: Prince Maccaus Publishers, 1983.

WYANDOT INDIANS

Connelley, William Elsey. *Wyandot Folk Lore*. Whitefish, MT: Kessinger Publishing, 2006.

*Libel, Autumn. *Huron: North American Indians Today*. Broomall, PA: Mason Crest Publishers, 2003.

SUICIDE

Blauner, Susan Rose. *How I Stayed Alive When My Brain Was Trying to Kill Me: One Person's Guide to Suicide Prevention*. New York: William Morrow, 2002.

Leone, Bruno, and David L. Bender, eds. *Suicide: Opposing Viewpoints*. San Diego: Greenhaven Press, 1998.

Quinnett, Paul G. *Suicide: The Forever Decision*. New York: Continuum, 1989.

INTERNET AND OTHER RESOURCES

THE NATIONAL ROAD

National Road/Zane Grey Museum
www.ohiohistory.org/places/natlroad

THE WYANDOT INDIAN NATION

Wyandot Nation of Kansas
www.wyandot.org

Native American Nations
www.nanations.com/wyandot/history.htm

TEEN SUICIDE

American Psychiatric Association
www.healthyminds.org

Suicide Awareness Voices of Education
www.save.org

American Foundation for Suicide Prevention

www.afsp.org

SafeUSA

www.safeusa.org

National Hopeline Network

1-800-SUICIDE

(1-800-784-2433)

National Suicide Prevention Lifeline

1-800-273-TALK

(1-800-273-8255)

TTY: 1-800-799-4889

ACKNOWLEDGMENTS

A huge thanks to the magicians at Candlewick Press: designers Sherry Fatla and Caroline Lawrence; copy editor Hannah Mahoney; and especially my wonderful editor, Liz Bicknell.

For ideas and inspiration, Kitty Suhar and the other young people at Walnut Creek Campus, in West Des Moines, Iowa: Barb Bailey-Mead, Spencer Bouma, Kyle "Styles" Connor, Sarah Eaton, Lorenzo García, Autumn Grismore, Patricia Hutchins, Josh Hutchinson, Fatima Kadic, Jessica Martin, and Kelce "Krickett" Prickett.

For interviews, ear-bending, manuscript reading, and advice: Alex Alford, Bob Falls, James Navé, Jane Anne Tager, Thomas Taggart, Kristen D. Taylor, George Teekel, Tom Tracy, Ginger West, Laurie Wolf, and Simon Wolf. Also Alan King at the National Road–Zane Grey Museum.

For their knowledge and advice regarding cars in general and Plymouth Barracudas in particular, thanks to Mike Wayne Byer, Mike William Byer, and Robert "Bruce" Barry of Mike Byer Auto and Truck Repair in Asheville, North Carolina.

For genealogical information on the Zane family, I'm very grateful to Diane J. Nichols. And for helping me in my attempt to solve the mystery of Miriam Zane, I must thank the Van Swearingen descendants Louise F. Johnson, Sharon Rouse Eye, and Mark Swearingen. Thanks also to the late Karel L. Whyte, foremost historian of the Swearingen/Van Swearingen family, and Katie Whyte, Karel's daughter, for making her mother's research available to me.

For providing a safe haven in which to write this book, I'm grateful to Beth & Tim Bates and to Beki Buchanan & Lin Orndorf at Outspoken in West Asheville, North Carolina.

AN AMAZING EXPEDITION TOLD THROUGH POETRY

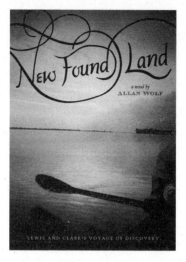

New Found Land
Lewis and Clark's Voyage of Discovery

Allan Wolf

**Winner of a Lion and the Unicorn Honor
for Excellence in North American Poetry**

★ "The dramatic effects of the expedition on the participants
come to life as they share their experiences and thoughts. . . .
Extraordinary and engrossing."
>—*School Library Journal* (starred review)

★ "In the flood of volumes marking . . . this epic journey,
Wolf manages something fresh and alive."
>—*Kirkus Reviews* (starred review)

Hardcover ISBN 978-0-7636-2113-1
Paperback ISBN 978-0-7636-3288-5

www.candlewick.com